ONCE HE BREAKS

CUBS FOR RENT #6

CHARITY PARKERSON

--Warning: This book is intended for readers over the age of 18.

Copyright © 2020 Charity Parkerson
Editor: Hercules Editing & Consultants
ISBN: 978-1-946099-63-1

INTRODUCTION

A SPOILED BILLIONAIRE MEETS A LOWLY RANCH
HAND AND SPARKS FLY... IN MORE WAYS
THAN ONE.

Dex Wise is the billionaire playboy everyone dreams of winning. Until they meet him, that is. Dex is spoiled and vain. The number of people he cares about can be counted on one hand and only takes one finger. He's never met anyone who doesn't have a price. Life bored him to tears years ago. The only things he feels any passion about are the TV shows he creates. Those are his babies. He won't let anything ruin that love, especially not the problems of some stubborn ranch hand named Colt who is way too sexy and stubborn for his own good.

When Colt started his job at Crooked Creek Ranch, he never expected his duties would include babysitting twenty drunk college students for some rich guy's reality show. While he might not have any choice in the matter, he'll be damned if he lets Dex Wise completely own him. If that means he has to sell his time through Cubs for Rent to free himself from the ranch that already owns him, then so be it. He just wished Dex wasn't so incredibly sexy. That seems a bit unfair.

When Dex makes Colt an offer he can't refuse, their passionate personalities don't disappear when Colt signs on the dotted line. But with the way they keep ending up in bed together, it is only a matter of time before someone breaks.

ONE

COLT FUCKING HATED this job so goddamn much and it grew in degrees of passion by the day. Becca was drunk. She was always drunk, so really, Colt wasn't surprised. That didn't make her any easier to deal with. As one of the last standing contestants of *Fresh Hell*—the reality show currently being filmed on the ranch where Colt worked— Becca had been flirting with him and disaster from day one. There were several problems with this. First, Colt was gay. Second, even if he weren't gay, Becca would have converted him. Third, and—oddly —most importantly, he loathed drunk people.

"I'm sorry. I just have to know." Becca snagged the tails of Colt's shirt and tugged, quickly unsnapping all the button snaps. The two halves fell open while Colt fought an eye twitch. Becca's light brown gaze moved down Colt's body. She looked disappointed. "More clothes. I should've known." She shook her head. "How do you wear all of this?" She gave a wave that screamed disgust toward Colt's clothing.

Sadly, Colt was getting used to this ridiculous behavior. He didn't bat an eyelash. "Some of us actually work for a living, which means getting down in the dirt. I dress appropriately. Do *not* touch me again."

A wicked-looking smile stretched Becca's lips. That was all the warning Colt got before Becca's hand swiped up and inside his shirt, smoothing over his abs. "Touch."

Colt leapt back out of her reach. "For fuck's sake. There has to be laws against this motherfucking bullshit. I've had all I can take of you spoiled-ass good-for-nothing..." Colt's cursing and muttering became indecipherable even to him as his stride ate up the ground between where Becca should have been mucking out stalls and Dex's trailer. This was all Dex Wise's fault, after all. Crooked Creek Ranch had been such a peaceful place once upon a time. Then Dex Wise had shown up with twenty drunken college students, a film crew, and his million-dollar trailer, and upended Colt's life. Instead of getting his regular duties accomplished each day, Colt found himself at Dex's mercy at all hours of the day. By one month in to filming the reality show, he had been looking for a way out. Now, nearly eight months in to Dex's constant presence, he was murderous. The ranch's owner, Clint, didn't give a fuck nothing was getting done around the ranch as long as Dex paid for disrupting the daily routine of things. He expected Colt would still handle the entire place on top of all this bullshit. Colt was done.

Colt threw open the trailer door without knocking. Dex had obviously been on his way out and they collided.

Dex looked damnably unfrazzled as he eyed Colt's open shirt. "More clothes. I should've known," he said, mirroring Becca's words.

Colt ignored the disappointment in Dex's voice and his words. "I swear to fucking Christ, Dex, if you don't get that drunk bitch out of my barn, I'll burn your goddamn trailer to the ground."

Dex curled his nose. "For the sake of ratings, I might let you, but seriously, don't you own like one decent shirt? I think we need to change your style."

"No. We're not talking about my style right now.

We're talking about the fucking she-devil you've unleashed upon my life."

Dex completely ignored his rage. As usual, he was completely unfazed by everything. "You don't get a say in this. It's time for you to own at least one shirt that just molds to those gorgeous abs of yours. Ratings are life."

Colt drew a slow and steady breath through his nose, trying to cling to the last threads of his sanity. He tried matching Dex's unaffected tone. "Filming is almost over. There's no point in changing my style now. Look, as close as I am to being free of this nonsense, you have to make that little girl go away from me or I can't be held responsible for my actions."

Dex waved away his words. "Actually, this is the perfect time for a wardrobe change. We need to make it look like the show's contestants weren't the only ones enriched by this experience. They got a little more mature and responsible while you loosened up a hair."

"No." Colt didn't even need to think about it. Dealing with these young and dumb people every day had done nothing but make Colt even more bitter and a little stupider. He worked his ass off for every little thing he owned. Colt wouldn't spend money he couldn't spare to make Dex's show look better.

"Yes. Let's go."

A snort escaped Colt with no input from his brain. "I know that you have no concept of actual work, but not only do I have to do that at some point today, I'm not spending my hard-earned funds because you had a whim."

Dex pulled the trailer door closed, as if Colt's protests were nothing more than background noise. "Clint has given me free rein over you so whatever my concept of work is, that's what you'll do. I'm buying you new clothes."

Colt's eye twitched. "I said no."

Sometimes, Dex would hold still and focus on Colt. In those moments, unexpectedly, the world would go silent. The anger would fall away. Dex's unusual grayish-blue gaze would fixate upon Colt. The muscle in his jaw would captivate Colt. Colt struggled to breathe properly as it happened now. The man possessed something Colt wished didn't affect him so strongly, but it did. Dex was powerful in some way Colt couldn't describe and it wasn't fair. "You're at my mercy, Colt." Fuck. He really was. A smile exploded across Dex's face, stealing the last of Colt's free will. Dex rarely smiled for real. "We're going to have so much fun. Plus, look on the bright side, I'm freeing you from Becca's clutches for a little while. I'm sure she'll be passed out by the time you get back."

As much as Colt hated to admit it, he needed a break from this place. If he stayed, one of two things would happen—he would either kill Becca or stroke out in his fury. Quitting wasn't even an option. Plus, as always, Colt's body automatically followed wherever Dex led. Dex had something no one else did. No doubt it had led to his success. Whatever it was, Colt wasn't as immune as he liked to think. That was scary as hell. Dex would leave him in the dust if Colt ever tipped his hand. People like Dex destroyed people like Colt. That was one truth that was universal. It was also already part of Colt's everyday reality. He needed things to be different.

COLT LANGLEY WAS SIX FEET FOUR INCHES AND two hundred and forty pounds of Texas born and raised sexy manliness. His boots were muddy. His cowboy hat matched the season and his hands were calloused. Eyes followed him everywhere he went because his hard body screamed hard labor and that was the kind of man who put his heart into every job, including sexual pleasure. Not to mention, his ass filled out a pair of Wranglers in a way that couldn't be ignored. Dex always got what he wanted and Dex had his sights set on Colt. Funnily enough, Colt seemed one hundred percent dead set against giving Dex a single inch. At first, Dex thought it was a game. After all, Colt wouldn't be the first to pretend disinterest to gain his attention. After months in Colt's everyday company, Dex had accepted the man truly wasn't interested. It was odd. That simply wasn't done. Even if someone didn't find him attractive, they couldn't resist his money. Yet Colt seemed to genuinely loathe the ground Dex walked on. That couldn't happen.

Dex pulled out his keys and motioned toward his car. "After you, Colton. As it turns out, I'd already asked Clint to find someone else to cover for you today before you barged in." Dex was about ninety percent sure Colt rolled his eyes but he turned his back too quickly for Dex to grab that other ten percent.

"My name isn't Colton." His grumbled words sounded childish. Dex's humor grew.

"Sure, it is. Colton Wayne Langley. Born in Uncertain, Texas on May fifth in nineteen eighty-seven. Your mom's name is Kate, your dad is Wyatt, and you have no siblings. Would you like me to keep going?"

Colt didn't look his way or say a word until they were strapped inside Dex's Bentley. "I could do the same, you know. Dexter Wise. Born in Topeka, Kansas on September twenty-third in nineteen seventy-nine. Your mom's name was Wendy and you don't have a dad. Would you like me to keep going?"

A chuckle that sounded evil even to Dex's ears slipped from his lips. "The funniest part of you trying to put me in my place is," Dex put the car in drive and took off so Colt wouldn't jump out. "that you had to Google me to learn all those details. Now, I wonder why you would do such a thing. It makes sense for me to investigate everyone working on my show, but you have no reason to look me up, unless..." Dex left it dangling there, taunting him.

Colt didn't take the bait. He was always ready for anything Dex threw his way. That was one of the reasons why Dex wanted him so badly. "I had to look you up because I had never heard of you before Clint announced you'd be taking over my life."

Dex didn't ease up. "Wow. You must have a photographic memory, then. That was months ago."

"I'm not sure what you're digging for here."

Even though Colt spoke in a bored tone, Dex could smell a lie a mile away. Colt wasn't dumb. He knew exactly what Dex was after. Dex wanted to fuck Colt. Own Colt. Dex needed a tiny nugget of hope that he had any shot at all, because Colt was hell to read. When Colt had been interested in Dex's best friend Wren, his eyes had flashed with heat and promise. When Colt looked at Dex, his eyes filled with annoyance and loathing. That shouldn't turn Dex on, but it did.

"Info," Dex finally said, answering Colt's question, and moving past how much Colt had already given away. "How did you end up at Crooked Creek?"

"How about this?" Colt said instead of answering. "I'll answer you if you agree to answer a question for me. If I'm going to be trapped with you all day, I shouldn't have to be under an inquisition all day too. This should be tit for tat."

"Fair enough." After all, Dex had nothing to hide.

"All right." Colt shifted positions, as if getting comfortable. "I grew up on a farm. It's all I know how to do. After a solid ten years of the rodeo circuit and going nowhere, I realized I had to settle down, but I had nowhere to call home. So I settled at Crooked

Creek. Why do you hire people to spend time with you?"

Dex chuckled at not only the half-ass answer but the quick-fire question. It seemed Colt was jumping in with both feet. "All right. No small talk questions from you, I see. I don't like to play games. It's like there's some unwritten rule that people have to date me and pretend to love me to get to my money. I don't have that kind of time. So let's skip the niceties. They want money. I want everything my way. Even trade. Why did you skip over becoming addicted to gambling and ending up over a hundred thousand dollars in debt before deciding to quit and get a real job?"

Silence filled the car, making Dex almost regret his words. Almost. If Colt couldn't be completely honest, then there was no reason for them to talk at all. Colt cleared his throat. It was an uncomfortable sound. "I know a lot of rodeo folks who would take offense to you calling out their profession as not being a real job, but I get your point. I wasn't making any real money doing it." He shifted positions again. It couldn't have been more obvious he wasn't comfortable with Dex for whatever reason. "As to the gambling, you left out that I'm also a recovering alcoholic, so really, I walked away from a lot of bullshit when I left the circuit. Everyone has to start over someplace. For me, a nice quiet ranch seemed like the perfect spot. I didn't count on it taking so long and I never expected you," Colt tacked on, sounding absent. "Where do you live anyhow? I know you can't stay in that trailer year-round."

Dex wanted time to mull over Colt's confessions, but he had agreed to exchange answers. "Actually, I could live in my trailer year-round, but I have a few homes. One is only about an hour away. That's where I live a majority of the time. I also have a place in New York, another in Malibu, and a cabin in Aspen. Oh, and I own a small private island for when I'm feeling like I need to soak up the sun and get away from the world."

"Jesus."

Dex ignored his horrified whisper. "What do you plan to do after you've paid off your debts with your Cubs for Rent money?"

He saw Colt's head whip his way from the corner of his eye. "How do you know about my Cubs for Rent job?"

Dex tsked. "You're losing the pace. It's my turn to ask a question. You answer and then you can ask another."

A sexy-sounding growl came from Colt's side of

the car. "I think I'd like to build a small place in the middle of nowhere and just enjoy the quiet. My life has been really loud and busy for a long time."

"Has it been loud, and you want it to be quiet? Or has it been hard, and you want it to be easy? Because those two aren't the same."

Colt snorted. "Who's messing up the order of things now?"

Dex waved off his words. "Yeah, yeah. I overheard you asking Wren how to get started with Cubs for Rent. I didn't know you actually planned to do it until I just made a stab in the dark. Now answer my question."

Colt didn't answer right away, as if he gave Dex's question some thought. "I guess I want it to be easier."

That was something Dex could fix. Maybe he would. After all, despite butting heads from the day they met, Dex couldn't stay away from Colt. There was something about the guy. Maybe he was worth saving.

TWO

THE STORE where they ended up was a place Colt hadn't known existed. Nothing had a price tag on it. There was also nothing there Colt would have chosen for himself, but Dex looked mildly pleased. In the end, Colt chose to stand still and let Dex hand him things. The pile in his arms got taller until a woman snagged him by the elbow and led him into a private room. It took him a moment to realize the huge space with coffee, water, a couch, and a chair was a dressing room. Actually, he might not have ever figured that out if Dex hadn't appeared and closed them inside. He sat down and demanded Colt to change, obviously intent on enjoying the show.

With a sigh, Colt went to work. He tried on three outfits with Dex sitting in complete silence.

His intense stare never wavered. He watched every move Colt made. At first, Colt felt awkward. His movements were stiff. After a while, his shoulders relaxed. He didn't think he looked right in anything he tried. Colt's reflection showed him a stranger in the designer jeans and lightweight V-neck t-shirts. Still, he kept at it. It wasn't until he wore a tux that fit like it had been tailor made that Dex finally came to his feet. He straightened Colt's bow tie and tugged on the jacket's tails as if forcing the piece into the perfect position. His gaze moved over Colt's body like he used an expert eye to judge him.

"This is more you than you've ever realized, I imagine." Before Colt could respond to that ludicrous statement, Dex changed the subject. "I have a genuine question. Then you can ask me one too, if you like—as we did earlier."

Colt's eyebrows crept toward his hairline. Dex sounded nervous, which was enough to raise Colt's curiosity to an all-time high. "All right."

"Why do you hate me?"

Considering Colt never expected to be hit with that question directly, he didn't know how to answer. An uncomfortable-sounding chuckle escaped him before he could stop it. "I don't think it's you in particular, and hate is a strong word. Maybe I'm just in the eat-the-rich stage of my life."

Dex's expression spoke volumes. He knew Colt was lying. "If you plan to work for Cubs for Rent, you need to get over that hill." Dex swiped his hands down Colt's chest, straightening the lapels of his jacket. "You'll be expected to smile and look the part of adoring arm candy." He looked genuine—like he cared, captivating Colt. "I'm not sure you have the acting abilities it takes to fake it. You're too free with your distaste. I don't think you can make someone undesirable feel wanted. Everything you feel shows on your face."

Colt knew he shouldn't take the bait. That didn't stop his hands from sliding across Dex's hips. He let his desire for the spoiled playboy show in his eyes. Colt took a step closer, completely invading Dex's space. "Maybe I should skip the middleman and seduce you instead. Why bother with Cubs for Rent when *the* Dex Wise is right here, within my grasp?"

Obviously deciding to call Colt's bluff, Dex's arms encircled Colt's neck. He closed the final inch between them. The instant Dex's body molded against Colt's, Colt's cock stirred. Dex smelled like a dream and fit perfectly against Colt's body. His cocky expression was the only thing stopping Colt from acting on his urge to taste Dex's full lips. Dex's voice turned sultry. "I don't think you're as dedicated to this game as you pretend."

"Try me." Even Colt heard the dare in his words.

A wicked-sounding chuckle slipped from Dex and vibrated against Colt's chest. "You want to skip Cubs for Rent and bypass the mildly wealthy horde to go for the big prize, huh? Okay. I'll play. How much do you make working at Crooked Creek?"

A hint of discomfort set in. He wasn't sure how far Dex would go. Plus, he looked crazy poor in comparison to Dex. "Twenty-eight thousand a year plus free housing. Another four thousand a year goes to paying off my debt to Clint."

Dex didn't scoff at the lowly amount, sparing Colt's pride. His hands moved to Colt's ass. "I'll pay you one hundred and fifty thousand a year to live with me and be completely at my mercy. I'd expect you to be—by all appearances—exclusive to me. You'd go where I go. Do what I want to do. What do you say? Are you truly ready for a new life?"

Temptation nearly took Colt's knees out. Never before had anyone spoken to life his dreams like Dex did. The shock had his mask slipping back into place. His heart retreated because that stupid organ was... well, stupid. A smile stretched Colt's lips that felt fake as hell. "And you said I couldn't make an undesirable person feel wanted."

Dex withdrew, taking all the happiness with him as he became the bored rich man once again. He stepped away from Colt. "It's not often I'm wrong, but I concede. You're ready to take on the mildly wealthy. You should try on the white dinner jacket too. There'll be times when you'll need that one."

Colt could barely breathe past the choking sensation of hurting Dex. While Dex was a good actor, Colt could feel him hiding his real self, and it was sucking the air from the room. Colt couldn't move or look away. He felt sick, knowing he had said such a thing. At some point in his life, he had become someone he no longer liked. He had allowed life to turn him bitter and cold. "I don't know why I said that."

Despite Dex's mouth lifting in one corner, he still didn't look at Colt directly. He worked on putting clothes into different piles. "I have no feelings to hurt."

That wasn't true in the least. Not that it would matter if his statement was true. At the end of the day, Colt had to live with himself. "If I thought your offer was genuine, I would accept."

Dex's gorgeous blue gaze slid back Colt's way

and locked on to him with an intensity that nearly had him taking a step back. "I meant every word, but I'm not sure you fully grasp what you would be agreeing to do."

The air felt thick. Colt's lungs struggled beneath the weight. "You want me to become your live-in whore."

The way Dex's nose curled had Colt fighting a smile. "Don't use that word. That's an archaic concept. You're an adult. If you choose to be my personal pet for your gain, then you're smart enough to recognize a great opportunity when you see it. But make no mistake, you would be my pet." Devilry flashed in Dex's eyes. "I can afford to give the best rewards for tricks well performed."

Damn. All Colt had to do was sign on the devil's dotted line. His entire life would be completely transformed in the blink of an eye. There was still a part of him that thought this was a bad joke. He imagined the moment he said yes, Dex would laugh at his stupidity for ever thinking Dex would pay him that much to warm his bed. In the end, Colt was a gambler all the way to his soul. "Okay."

Dex's expression transformed into the serious version Colt was used to seeing. "If you choose this, there's no backing down."

Colt nodded. He got that. "I'm in. Just tell me where to sign." His tone matched his mindset. Colt liked Dex in the only ways it mattered. He would give the man his time and body. After all, in all honesty, Colt had lost his soul a long time ago, and he had done a lot more for less.

Triumph etched Dex's features, stealing the air from Colt's lungs. "You definitely need to try on the white jacket as well, then. I have an event to attend at the end of next week. I'll call Clint and tell him to replace you."

Colt dipped his chin in agreement. It was too late to turn back now, and he had to start giving in somewhere. It may as well be here.

EVEN THOUGH DEX WAS KNOWN TO MAKE THE occasional impulse buy, Colt would never be on that list. From the moment he learned Colt would be working for Cubs for Rent, it had been Dex's plan to throw money Colt's way until the man was so enamored by him that he had no choice but to land in Dex's bed. This was better. Dex didn't like waiting. He wasn't the type to woo someone. People usually fell at Dex's feet. Of course, it wasn't because they couldn't resist Dex. His money was orgasmic, apparently. Dex wasn't the type to balk.

There was something different about Colt. From the first moment they met, Colt had barely suppressed his dislike, and—for once—Dex didn't believe it was a game. In the past, when someone hoped they could win him by pretending disinterest, they had always done something to give themselves away. Usually, they realized Dex gave no fucks about anyone, so they were wasting their time faking it. Colt genuinely disliked Dex, and it was fascinating. It seemed the key to prying open Colt's mind was straightforwardness. Dex made an offer. Colt accepted. Let the games begin. Also, goddamn, Colt had a body to die for, and Dex loved every minute of watching him try on clothes.

Eight months ago, Dex had shown up at Crooked Creek needing to spend a couple of months learning all there was to know about the place so he could create the perfect challenges for his contestants. Clint had immediately thrown Dex Colt's way. Colt had taken one look at Dex and decided Dex would be nothing but in his way. That had pretty much been their story ever since. Through twenty-two weeks of once a week live voting, days of filming while hoping to make it seem like less time passed than actually had, and countless complaints on Colt's part, they had been destined to end up here. Together. Dex couldn't wait until Colt looked at him without an ounce of hatred. It had to happen. Dex had never wanted anyone more than the bitter cowboy.

Dex handed the woman who had been helping them all morning his black card and paid for Colt's clothes before Colt could learn the price. Price didn't matter to Dex. He imagined it would to Colt. Since Colt had agreed to be his exclusively, while Colt changed into a set of new clothes—on Dex's order, of course—Dex had taken care of some business. First order, getting close to sixty new outfits delivered to his estate near San Antonio. He wouldn't move Colt to his trailer on the ranch for two reasons—filming was almost over, and he wouldn't humiliate Colt in front of his former co-workers. That last bit brought on a few more items of business. He called Clint first and dropped the news Colt would not be returning—ever. Next was Toby from Cubs for Rent. They needed to take Colt off their site. He also called his lawyer. While Dex had him on the phone, he got the man started on paying off all Colt's old debts. Dex couldn't have that hanging over Colt's head, distracting him. With everything in order, Dex focused on Colt. He was sexy as sin in a way that normally didn't appeal to Dex. He was wide-shouldered and tall. He took up too much space and was rough around the edges. Colt wouldn't be tamed and that thought alone made Dex's mouth water. No doubt, Colt would taste wild and take it hard. He was delectable. If he turned out to be tiresome, Dex would send him on his way—debts paid and richer for the wear. No harm done. Dex could afford the risk.

Colt looked like a new man when he appeared outside the dressing room—sort of. Dex bit back a sigh at the sight of his cowboy hat. He held it between his hands, obviously intent on putting it back on his head the moment they stepped outside. Dex supposed he could concede one point.

He stood. "Are you ready to see your new home?"

Colt didn't exactly shift nervously. It was more of a questioning shuffle. "I'm moving today?"

"Of course," Dex said with a shrug. "My attorneys have started on the paperwork. Clint knows you won't be returning, and I'll get my assistant to handle gathering your things. Oh," Dex added as if he almost forgot. "I paid off the seventy grand you still owed Clint that kept you beholden to him. I can't have that. You're mine now. Just call it a sign-on bonus."

"Oh." He twirled his hat, looking like a fast-moving train nearly mowed him down. "Thank you." He cleared his throat. "You know I'm new at this, so I don't really know what to say to that."

Dex shook his head while fighting a smile. He hadn't been this happy in a long time. Colt was a treasure and didn't know it. "I think I need to ask Wren to help you get settled. Your life is easier now. Just keep that in mind." Dex headed out with Colt on his heels. He knew Colt would follow.

"I like Wren."

Pride grew in Dex's chest as he tossed a bag of clothes inside the car. Everyone liked Wren. He was sparkly and flirtatious. Wren was also kinky as fuck, but Dex would never get to taste that again. They were still best friends, but Wren had met his other half. While Dex was happy for him, in hindsight, he wished he would have married Wren immediately, keeping Wren for himself. Everyone else in the world paled in comparison and hated Dex. Not that Dex cared about that last part. His TV creations were his one and only love. Creating an escape from reality by showcasing a hot mess of reality shows was an addiction for Dex. His heart would never be free enough to satisfy a lover. There was no soul mate out there for him. The art of film was his other half. Their marriage had served him well. Saved him. No person could compete.

Dex waited to respond until they were buckled inside the car. "I'll call him for you later." He looked over at a nervous-looking Colt, and—for a moment— he worried he had snipped the wings from the thing that fascinated him about Colt. He didn't want to break him or tame him. "You should probably throw that hat away."

Colt's eyes flashed with rebellion. "You should probably go fuck yourself."

A chuckle rose in Dex's throat. He put the car in drive. "There's the sexy cowboy I know and love. I knew you were still in there somewhere." With a smile that felt permanent stretching his lips, Dex settled in for the long drive home. They would be great together.

UNLIKE THE TRIP TO THE CLOTHING STORE, THE drive to Dex's was made in companionable silence with only the occasional spatter of conversation. Truthfully, they didn't have a lot in common besides hardheadedness. Despite that, Colt was interested in Dex's life. He imagined it had been an adventure. By the time Colt worked up the nerve to ask, Dex pulled into the driveway of the single most gorgeous house he had ever seen. All of his questions died on his lips. Instead, Colt found himself fighting the urge to babble like an idiot in the face of so much wealth. In theory, he had known Dex was a billionaire. He had been inside the man's ridiculously extravagant trailer on set, but this was different. This wasn't a home. It was an estate. He felt... small. Colt couldn't think of another way to describe how he felt in the face of so much.

As one of the multi-garage doors opened and Dex pulled inside, Colt caught a glimpse of the pool behind the house. It was massive. That was all he knew from the brief peek.

"I have an extra set of keys somewhere inside. I'll make sure you get them before I leave."

Leave. There was some new information in that sentence. Not that Dex had told him much beyond saying Colt belonged to him now. Colt was pretty used to going with the flow. It was like that while spending years on the road. He had always been ready to go to whichever town had the next event with the biggest possible pot. A small part of him missed that life and was giddy at the idea of sleeping in a different bed tonight. The rest of Colt was in complete shock and slightly terrified. That didn't mean he planned to stop.

Colt followed Dex inside the house, doing his best not to look at everything like he had never seen a house before in his life. The door they entered led into a mudroom. It was empty. There were no shoes, jackets, or hats of any kind. There was no time like the present to make his mark. Colt hung his cowboy hat on the first empty wooden peg they came to.

Dex looked his way with pride in his eyes. "You're officially home now."

A chuckle escaped Colt. "I have to start somewhere."

Dex's expression turned sweet, stealing Colt's breath. "Good choice. Come on. I'll find those keys for you and then I'll make arrangements with Wren to have your truck brought to you. Not that you'll be stuck here in the meantime," Dex said, heading through the kitchen. "I'll make sure you have the keys to one of the other cars in the garage too."

It didn't sound like Dex intended to stay long. Colt tried to force his eyes on his surroundings as Dex led him through the house. Everything was clean and the place even smelled like money, but

Colt's eyes kept latching on to Dex and refusing to budge. He was different today, for the most part. While Dex was still demanding and abrasive, he had shown some weaknesses and peeks of other almost human-like qualities. Adding these new facets on top of his looks was sucking Colt in a little. They cleared the door of a massive bedroom. It was big enough to be a house he would love to own. The walls were light—almost too bright with the sun from all the windows hitting them. Colt looked harder at them, trying to see why. It looked like there were tiny accents of silver swirled through the white paint, making the room seem even bigger. The comforter on the bed was a duller silver. Everything looked huge and expensive. Untouched. As Colt took in the cherry wood bed, dresser, and nightstands, Dex moved to a door inside the room. He opened the door and Colt caught a peek of a room that was almost as big as the one he currently occupied. It took him a moment to realize it was the closet. Dex tossed Colt's bag of new clothes inside and took off his shirt. Then Colt saw nothing else. His gaze locked on the muscles in Dex's back. He loved a sexy back. Colt couldn't explain it.

"This is our bedroom," Dex said over his shoulder as he changed shirts. "There's a cleaning lady that comes twice a week, so feel free to jerk off on our sheets; she'll change them." He winked at Colt as he turned and dragged his shirt down, covering the delicious skin Colt wanted to stare at all day. "My attorney will come by tomorrow with some paperwork for you to sign. Keep an eye out for that. What am I forgetting?" Dex looked thoughtful for a second. "Oh, keys." He headed back out of the bedroom, leaving Colt to follow.

Colt didn't say a word until they stepped inside what was obviously Dex's office. There were awards and the room smelled like wood.

"Do you not intend to stay even a few minutes?"

Dex circled a huge desk and dug through the drawers. He came out with two sets of keys. Both rings had remotes on them. "Not tonight, gorgeous. I have to get back to the ranch. You know I'm a hoverer. If I don't keep a close eye on my creations, the directors will screw them up. I'll be back and forth, so—in the meantime—I don't want you trapped." He handed the keys to Colt. "One set is for the house, alarm, etc. and the other is for the Range Rover in the second bay. Oh." He pulled out his wallet. "I don't know what's in the fridge, but here." He pulled several bills from his wallet and held them out to Colt. "Take this in case you need anything.

This is your home now. Please feel free to acquaint yourself with it."

Colt eyed the money but didn't take it. "I'm not completely broke. I can afford food."

Dex smirked and stepped closer. Colt was so enamored by the cockiness in Dex's eyes that he didn't move fast enough before Dex shoved the money in the pocket of his jeans. He didn't pull his hand back out. Instead, he took another step closer until there was barely any space between them.

Dex's gaze never wavered from Colt's. "Rule one. Never turn down my money. You'll soon realize it means next to nothing to me."

A hint of the irritation he always felt around Dex came roaring back. "Only someone with an endless supply of funds would say something like that."

Colt's words seemed to roll right off Dex. He shook his head. "Actually, most rich people I know believe their money is everything. Don't get me wrong, I like being rich, but it's only a byproduct of my real love." He wiggled his fingers, reminding Colt he still held Colt's pocket. "So don't complain when I give you more than agreed upon."

It was like Colt couldn't stop. "You do too much. It makes me uncomfortable."

Dex finally pulled his hand from Colt's pocket,

but he grabbed two handfuls of ass instead of backing away. He spun and Colt found himself trapped between Dex and the desk. Dex massaged, moving higher until his hands were beneath Colt's shirt. The lower halves of their bodies met. Dex was hard for him. Colt's mouth went dry and his body immediately reacted in kind.

"You haven't seen uncomfortable yet with me." His hands kept moving higher, dragging Colt's shirt up until his thumbs stroked Colt's nipples. Colt was turned on to the point of being frozen in place. He tried not to pant as he waited to see what Dex would do next. A calculating look passed over Dex's features. It fascinated Colt. "You're not ready to stop hating me yet. I'll see you in a few days." He stepped away. "Call me if you need anything before then."

Colt watched Dex leave with his heart in his throat. He didn't know how to say he didn't hate Dex. In truth, Colt didn't know why he couldn't loosen up with Dex around. Maybe he thought Dex would end up being just like every other rich guy Colt had ever met. Colt didn't want to end up one hundred thousand dollars indebted and working the land of yet another asshole he hadn't been able to resist.

Arousal had Dex's skin feeling too tight. He tried breathing through the lust as he pushed the button on his steering wheel to call Wren. For a few months, Wren had worked on call with Cubs for Rent, stealing his time from Dex. Dex had been forced to pull out the big guns to steal Wren back. He had decided to give Wren something he couldn't resist—a legitimate job that didn't require him dating anyone other than his husband. It had taken Dex two solid weeks to convince Wren to take the job as his assistant. Once Wren realized he would have a normal and set schedule plus vacation time and the best boss on the planet, Wren had given in gracefully. Actually, he had thrown his hands up and growled, accepting that Dex wouldn't take no for an answer. Either way, Dex had Wren back at his side and in his line of sight, so he knew his best friend was properly cared for—as he deserved.

"Hello?"

A rare smile pulled at the corners of Dex's mouth as the sound of Wren's voice filled the car. "Hey, fire sprite. I made a big purchase today and I need you to handle some things for me."

Wren didn't hesitate. "Of course. Hit me with

the list."

There was no one else Dex trusted like he trusted Wren. "I need you to head out to the ranch. You'll need boxes and boxing tape. Sorry, but I don't know how much. You might have to go assess things and then buy what you need."

"Ranch, boxes, and tape. Check. What did you buy at the ranch?"

"Colt." Dead air met Dex's announcement. He tried waiting for Wren's reaction. Dex didn't make it. "Are you still there?"

Wren cleared his throat. "Yeah. I was just... yeah. So I take it I'm packing up Colt's things."

"That's why I love you. You make my life easy. Yes. Pack up his things and toss them in the back of his truck. When you're done, please deliver everything—truck and all—to my place. I just dropped Colt off so he can get used to his new circumstances without anyone staring at him. So, probably wait until tomorrow to deliver his things." An idea hit Dex. "Oh, I know, have Haven and Finch follow you over there and Finch can go swimming. It's been a while since he's been out to the house."

A tired-sounding chuckle filled the car. "You always know exactly how to twist me around your finger. I'll get it done, sweetie. But," Wren said, dragging out the word. "You have to sit still for five minutes later and tell me what's going on."

Dex couldn't stop smiling. He loved Wren. Wren might work for him, but he never stopped being Dex's friend before everything else. "No need for digging or confessions. I want him, so I acquired him. You know I always get what I want."

"All right," Wren said, completely accepting Dex as normal, even though they both knew he wasn't.

"I love you." The words popped from Dex. Wren was the only person on the planet who heard those three words from him. He was the only one who deserved them.

"I love you too, angel. I'll take care of everything. You know you can count on me."

He did know it. If Dex knew nothing else, he knew Wren would never fail him. If Dex lost everything tomorrow, Wren would still be there. There was no one else on the planet who wouldn't abandon Dex in the blink of an eye if he wasn't rich. There was a tugging in his gut, though. Dex recognized something in Colt—something he had only ever seen in Wren. Saving Wren was the best decision Dex had ever made. He hoped—one day—he could say the same for Colt.

THREE

CLINT: *How dare you walk away in the middle of the day without a word to me?*

For a long moment, Colt stared at his phone, scared to breathe. He had belonged to Clint for so long. What if he burned this bridge and Dex changed his mind? Fuck it. He had to get this over with. Colt couldn't live with this shadow over his head. He was already fifteen minutes in to breathing with his head between his knees because he had obviously lost his goddamn mind accepting Dex's offer. Colt couldn't go back to Crooked Creek. He couldn't spend another damn day trapped under Clint's thumb. Nobody knew. Dex had to be better. He wrapped his soul-deep hatred of Clint around his heart and replied.

Colt: *Did you get paid?*

Clint: *That's beside the point. You know damn well this isn't about the money.*

But it was. At least, it was to Colt. Colt blocked Clint's number. It felt good. Damn. It felt way better than he ever imagined. The immediate weight that lifted from Colt's shoulders had him coming to his feet and sucking a deep breath of free air. Even if Dex changed his mind, Clint had been paid. Colt didn't have to go back. He didn't know what to do first. His first reaction was to celebrate, but Clint had alienated him from all his friends years ago and Dex was gone. His truck was still at the ranch. He looked down at the keys he had dropped on the coffee table when hyperventilation hit earlier while he had been checking out the house. Apparently, there was a Range Rover somewhere. Colt dug out the bills Dex had stuffed in his pocket. He flipped through them. Seven hundred dollars. Jesus. He had seven hundred dollars in his hand and a free ride. Colt could go do anything. He glanced around the quiet living room. Everything was leather, wood, and marble. It was clean and smelled like apples for some reason. Colt shoved the money in his pocket and sat back down. The plush leather welcomed him. He spotted a remote on the table. Colt snagged it and started pressing buttons. First, the fireplace fired to life. Colt turned it off. It was too hot outside for that. After a few more tries, the TV above the fireplace switched on. He eyed it for a minute. Dex was the TV god. It seemed strange that he had a TV that was probably only forty-eight inches. Colt looked around. In fact, the whole room looked unused. When Dex had left, Colt had simply turned away from the office and stumbled from room to room until the panic struck.

Colt stood. He trailed from room to room again, searching for Dex's true space. Colt didn't know how he knew Dex never went in that other room, he just did. There was a tugging in Colt's gut. He knew he would know Dex's space when he came to it. Colt headed back to the bedroom Dex said they now shared. He had noticed several doors when they had been in there earlier. Now, he was beyond curious where they led. For a moment, he eyed the huge bed again. It looked like a cloud. He was oddly excited to try it, but not yet. The closet door was the only door on the right side of the room. There were three doors to the left. The first one was a smaller closet. It was empty. The second was the bathroom. For a solid five minutes, Colt stared into that room. An enormous tub sat in the center, looking like something out of a dream. Parties could be thrown in Dex's bathroom.

Colt could picture Dex with champagne in one hand and five gorgeous men piled in the water with him. Colt turned away from the image.

He tried the third door. The moment it swung wide, the scent of leather washed over him. Even though it was daytime, the room was pitch black. Colt felt around until he found a light switch. When the room lit, Colt froze in awe.

"Holy shit." He dragged out every syllable as he eyed the man cave. Colt had definitely found Dex's space. It was a theater. Full wall projector. Leather recliner theater-style seating. A drink and snack bar at the back. Five fucking Emmys sat on the bar like they were just trinkets. Colt had no words. Reality hit Colt like a ton of bricks. There was no reason for him to be here. Dex was so far out of Colt's reach, they weren't even in the same stratosphere. It was funny how he had been hovering on the edge of Dex's wealth for months but seeing this one space was a switch being thrown on the magnitude of Dex's stardom. Dex was mad talented and probably stalked by countless actors who would kill to win him. People way better than Colt. Colt was no one. Yet, he was here. It was... terrifying.

It had been the longest day in the history of days. Becca had been passed out when Dex had gotten back from taking Colt home. Unfortunately, that hadn't lasted long before she was up and ready to kill Colt for leaving her actual work to do. It seemed she had gotten used to spending her time drinking while she flirted with Colt and he did her work. It also seemed she had believed he had let it go on because he enjoyed her flirting. Dex found it odd that she had never once considered the ranch had to continue running with or without her help, and someone would have to do what she refused to do. The place wasn't run on magic. It only seemed that way because Colt was so amazing. After a few hours of dealing with Becca's bullshit without Colt as a buffer, Dex was done. He couldn't wait to lock himself away in silence for the rest of the night.

"You stole my employee."

Dex stared longingly at the door of his trailer. He had almost made it. Dex had been mere seconds away from taking off his shoes and calling Colt. Fuck. He turned and pasted on his most obnoxious smirk.

"Hello, Clint. How may I help you?"

Rage flashed in the man's amber-colored eyes. He was big like Colt. Most likely, he had worked the land he owned at some point before hitting it big on racehorses. Clint ate up the space between them before hovering so close, his cowboy hat nearly took out Dex's eye.

"You heard me, boy. You stole Colt, knowing damn well he's the only one who keeps this place going."

Boy? Dex's fake smile kicked up a notch, because he knew Clint would hate it. "Unless you've been fucking Colt, I didn't steal him from you. We're dating. I didn't like him working, so I ensured he no longer needed to do so."

Clint blinked—like Dex spoke a foreign language. For a moment, he floundered. "Why would you think... I'm straight, asshole. It's just that... I mean, you disrupted my entire team. This ranch depends on dependable people."

"Really? People? As in more than one?" Even Dex heard the disbelief in his voice. "I have to say, I've been here eight months and the only person I've seen doing anything at all is Colt. Yet you have a team of men who could be working if they'd stop fucking all the college girls that are here to compete." Clint looked ready to have an aneurysm. He was apoplectic. Dex didn't back down. "Ranch hands are a dime a dozen. If you'd like, I can get my assistant to find you a new one."

Clint's huge chest heaved, making Dex wonder if he was about to be in a fight for the first time in his adult life. "I don't need your goddamn assistant to do my hiring."

Dex shrugged. "All right. Then, did you need something else?" It was obvious Clint wanted to demand Dex bring back his slave. But Clint couldn't do it, because then he would have to admit he was in fact gay, and he had been keeping Colt indebted to him so he could fuck Colt on the sly with zero concerns about getting called out. The man had no idea how observant Dex could be, and—with his money—he could find anything out. Plus, Clint simply wasn't as slick as he liked to think. Dex waited. He was oddly curious what Clint would do next.

"This isn't over."

Sigh. Dex would have to find a new place to film this show if it got renewed next year. Or maybe he would pull out and let someone else back this one. No matter what he decided, Dex wouldn't be back here after the season finale. "Have a nice night, Clint." Without looking back, Dex headed inside. He locked the door behind him and took a breath.

Dex had known he was starting shit by stealing Colt. That was the real reason he had taken Colt straight home and left him. On some visceral level, he had needed to make the bullshit stop once he had learned what made Colt hate everyone. Dex only had one superpower. It was money. Sometimes, he used it for good. As he dug out his phone, he recognized his motives might not be as altruistic as he liked to believe, because he wanted Colt, and he didn't want Clint to have him.

Dex: *Are you awake?*

Colt: *Yes. I found your theater room and I'm catching up on all the movies I've missed.*

An intense wave of happiness washed over Dex just seeing Colt's name appear on his phone. He hit the call icon and pressed the device to his ear as he moved to his bedroom. It rang twice.

"Hello?"

"Hello, sexy cowboy. How many movies have you seen today?"

"I believe I'm on number five. I've also raided your fridge, tried out your humongous tub, and searched for your porn and naughty toy collection, which is oddly nonexistent."

Dex chuckled as he fell across his bed. "Why is that odd? I don't have time for porn."

"How does someone not have time for porn? Do you spend hours critiquing it?"

Dex didn't hesitate. "Of course."

A sexy laugh caressed his ear. "I'm only teasing," Colt said, sounding tired and sexy. "I didn't search your house."

"It's your house now too." Dex closed his eyes and took a deep breath. He let his muscles relax. "Speaking of which, I believe I've made an enemy of Clint. It seems you're the only one who works around here, and he didn't appreciate losing you."

"I'll bet." The bitterness in Colt's voice was thick. Dex imagined he would feel the same, but Colt didn't know how much Dex knew about the situation and he wanted to keep things that way.

"Was there anything in the fridge to raid?"

"Not really, but honestly, I hated to drive the Range Rover. If anything happened to it, I couldn't afford to fix it."

Dex blew out a sigh. He didn't know how to make Colt stop feeling like a guest. "It's insured and it needs to be driven. I can't imagine it's good for the engine for it to just sit like it does." An idea hit him. "Actually, you'd be doing me a huge favor if you took it out and picked up some groceries while you're out. Just whatever you want or like to eat. Wren is coming by tomorrow with your things. He'll have Finch with him, and you know how kids love snacks. There's nothing there for him. Lately, my house hasn't felt much like a home. It needs life and care."

"Don't worry. I'll take care of everything."

With his eyes closed, Dex reveled in the sound of Colt's voice. "I know you will. Despite what you think of me, I have noticed how much effort you put into everything you do."

An irritated growl caressed his ear. "I don't think badly of you. It's just that... ugh. I don't know how to explain it, but I don't dislike you, okay?"

"I don't dislike you either," Dex said, incapable of suppressing a smile. It faded away. "I know I have some cold and calculating ways, but as a stipulation of our continued friendship, Wren has made me promise to use my words more often. So I'm really glad you're there, even though I miss seeing you here." Silence met his confession, making Dex wonder if he had shocked Colt speechless. Maybe he was better off not using his words.

Finally, Colt cleared his throat. "Well, if we're confessing things, then I have to admit I'm still not sure what to think of this deal or why you made it, but—for now—I have no regrets."

That was high praise coming from Colt. Dex

would take it. "On that note, I will say good night. I'm not sure yet what day I'll be home, but it won't be long."

"You know how to reach me."

Colt sounded like he was smiling. It was strange that such a small thing made him happy, but it did. "Same."

"Goodnight, gorgeous."

Dex's excitement grew as he disconnected the call. He would give Colt a few days of peace. Colt had earned them. Then the real seduction would begin. He couldn't wait to see Colt's shock firsthand. A chuckle escaped Dex as he pressed the phone to his chest. He couldn't wait to see Colt period.

FOUR

COLT WAS SURPRISINGLY busy for someone who no longer worked. Driven by an unexpected need to make Dex's life better, Colt dove into giving Dex's home the life he claimed it needed. He had taken the Range Rover out and to the grocery store first thing. From there, Colt kept finding more and more little things. His clothes arrived from the store. Colt wanted to hang them in the empty bedroom closet, only to realize there were no hangers. So he had gone back out. Each time he noticed something missing that a normal person would own—like dish soap—Colt found himself back in the car and down the road. In fact, he made so many trips, he almost forgot about Wren coming with his things until Wren came through the door.

"Don't panic. It's just me. I have keys."

Colt poked his head inside the mudroom and caught sight of Wren hauling in a box while trying to close the door behind him.

"Hey." Colt rushed to relieve him of his load. He set it aside, since there was nothing in the mudroom anyhow. "It's good to see you. I thought your brother was coming too."

Wren pointed toward the back of the house. "Haven is taking him swimming so he doesn't get bored. When Dex built this house, he had a wheelchair to pool lift installed for Finch. Now Finch wants to come over all the time. I guess, eventually, I'll have to break down and get a pool too."

Colt didn't know what to say. He couldn't imagine Dex doing such a thing, but then again, he was beginning to think he had not only misjudged Dex but knew nothing about him at all. That did explain why the house seemed to be wheelchair friendly. Just subtle things, but still. "That sounds like fun. If you'd like, you can go too. As I'm sure you saw, I don't have much. I traveled for so many years on the rodeo circuit, and only stayed in furnished places when I sat still, so there's like clothes and stuff. That's really it. I can get all that myself."

Wren waved off his words. "It'll go faster with two of us working on it. By the way, your old boss Clint is a real dick. Do you know, he allotted me exactly two hours to gather your things? Thankfully, as you said, you don't have a lot of stuff because he stood over my shoulder the whole time like he expected I would steal everything not nailed down."

Nothing about any of that surprised Colt. He couldn't say that without opening a topic he didn't want to discuss. "Sorry about that."

Wren shrugged. "It's not a big deal." He flashed Colt a devilish smile. "I'm used to men watching my every move." Before Colt could fall victim to Wren's charms, Wren motioned toward the door. "Let's get your stuff inside, and then you can come meet Finch. Haven says he hyped him up on the way here, so now he's super excited to meet a real cowboy."

A chuckle slipped from Colt. "He'll be disappointed."

"I don't know," Wren said, heading for the door. "You haven't disappointed me yet and I'm a much tougher audience than he is." He glanced Colt's way as they stepped outside. "It's funny, though. You don't look like a cowboy today. This is the first time I've seen you in anything other than Wranglers and a twill western shirt."

Colt fought a blush. "Dex said I couldn't wear those things anymore."

Wren rolled his eyes. "He'll change his mind. Dex is like that. He'll buy you a bunch of new stuff because he wants to spoil you, but then he'll beg you to wear your old stuff, because that's the person he liked enough to spoil. You'll get used to the whiplash. On a serious and similar note, I was floored to hear the news. I thought you two hated each other."

While grabbing a box from the back of his truck, Colt tried to think of an answer that didn't sound batshit insane. He couldn't explain to someone like Wren what it was like to be him. A loud and happy-sounding squeal rent the air, reminding Colt that Finch was at the pool. His tongue loosened. Wren's life wasn't as easy as he made people believe. Colt had a feeling that Wren was just a much better actor than him. "It's not that I hate Dex," Colt said after a minute. He waited until Wren had a box too and they were headed back inside to continue. "I guess I dislike people like him—more money than they'll ever need while the rest of us struggle for things they'll never understand. Things have always been a challenge for me, and he doesn't seem like anything has ever been difficult for him. It makes it hard to connect with him, I guess."

They kept up a steady conversation while making several trips for more boxes. "If it helps," Wren said, after obviously thinking over Colt's words. "Dex's life hasn't been easy. I won't betray his trust and say more, but he earned every dime he's made, and he paid with his soul. That's why he's so free with his money when it comes to people like you and me. Just watch him with your heart and not your eyes, and I promise Dex will amaze you. He pisses me off sometimes, because he obsesses over things to the point of making everything worse most of the time. There are reasons for that, and—where it counts—he's pretty fantastic. I'm glad you're giving him a shot."

"I'm not sure I had a choice," Colt admitted with a chuckle.

Wren laughed. The sound made Colt smile. "That makes total sense to me. I've never been able to stand against Dex either. Obviously," he said, dropping his box in Dex's bedroom. A hint of jealousy hit Colt out of nowhere. Wren knew where Dex's bedroom was without being told and that fact suddenly dawned on Colt. Dex's house had been built to accommodate Wren's brother—like he thought Wren might live here someday. Colt stuffed it down. He had no right to feel any sort of way about anything. This was a job. Colt tried for a smile as he realized Wren watched him in silence. Wren shook his head. It was like he read Colt's mind. "Don't start down that path. Dex and I love each other as friends."

In his aggravation at himself, Colt tried for innocence. "What? I never said otherwise. Plus, I'm just an employee."

Wren snorted. "Don't play dumb. Dex could've set you up anywhere. Instead, he moved you into his home. He's never done that before. You're more than an employee, and I feel certain you know it. I can see it in your eyes. You feel something you don't want to feel." Wren stepped around him and headed down the hall. "Come on. Let's finish this so we can enjoy the day. Otherwise, I might stand here and psychoanalyze you all day."

Colt didn't move right away. Instead, he stared at the bed he had slept in alone. It was Dex's bed. Colt couldn't pretend it hadn't immediately felt like his too. According to Wren, Dex had never moved anyone else into this house. Wren would know. Colt wished that knowledge didn't fuck with him so much. Dex wasn't the first rich man to try to break Colt with promises of a better life. Colt never ended up being the one living better. He needed to remember that and protect his heart this time. Nothing good came from loving a rich man.

Confusion kept Dex moving from room to room. Colt was nowhere to be found. Finally, he gave up and backtracked until he found the tiny brunette who cleaned two days a week.

"Have you seen my man?"

She flashed him a smile. "Hello, Mr. Wise. He's out back."

Dex's eyebrows rose. "Is he by the pool? I looked out and didn't see him."

She moved to the window and glanced through the pane. "He's right there," she said, pointing to a spot to the left of the pool.

Dex moved to join her at the window and peered out. Following the line of her finger, he spotted a light-colored blanket beneath a tree. Colt was sprawled out across it. Dex gave her a nod. "Thank you." Without another word, Dex cut through the kitchen and out the French doors. In a matter of minutes, he stood over the giant cowboy he had missed more than he ever realized was possible. An out-of-control wave of happiness washed over

Dex as he stared down at Colt. "What are you doing?"

The sexiest grin Dex had ever seen curved Colt's lips. His eyes opened. The blue gaze that captured him months ago locked on to Dex. "I'm an outdoorsy type guy. The sun is shining. I had to find a way to enjoy it."

Dex cast a look around the backyard. "Did you see the lawn chairs and lounges that cost a small fortune? They were meant for just this endeavor. In fact, there's a pool and everything."

Colt patted the blanket beside him. "This is better. Come check it out. I promise the grass is so much more comfortable than any lawn chair."

He couldn't resist Colt's offer. There was no hatred on his face today. Dex dropped to his knees before settling onto his back beside Colt. The leaves above his head danced in the slight breeze while sparkles of sunlight peeked between each one. While the blanket and grass combination beneath him wasn't horrible, Dex still didn't love it. The sensation of softened prickles against his skin had him taking slow breaths to fight being triggered. He had a problem with weird sensations against his skin. Colt had no reason to know that, so Dex tried sucking it up.

To give himself something else to focus on, Dex rolled to his side, pillowed his head with his arm, and stared at Colt. "What have you done with your time while I've been gone?" Dex didn't add that he had missed Colt being on location. He hadn't realized until he hadn't seen Colt's face every day how much he had come to depend on Colt being there.

Colt turned his head. His blue gaze held Dex's stare. "More than you'd think. I expected I would get bored doing nothing all day. Instead, I realized how much I don't get accomplished every day because I'm always too busy. I got to wash my truck. Do you know how long it's been since I got to detail and wax my truck? Ages," he said without waiting for Dex to answer.

Dex fought the urge to tell him he should have paid someone else to do it. Instead, he went with keeping Colt smiling. "What else did you do?"

"You're smiling."

He was, but Dex didn't know why Colt pointed it out. "I'm enjoying myself. What else did you do?"

For a moment, Colt simply stared at him in silence before shaking his head and continuing. "I finally met Wren's brother. We swam and I wore my cowboy hat for him, since he had never met a cowboy. He's a cool kid."

"He's had a great brother as an example."

Colt's expression turned serious. "It's odd. You really love Wren. I thought he was like a possession to you or something when we first met, but the more I learn, the more I realize I don't know you at all."

Dex shrugged off Colt's claim. "Maybe he is a possession to me. I like owning beautiful things."

"Is that why I'm here?"

Colt still looked serious—like Dex's answer mattered. Dex knew there was a right and wrong response here. He just didn't know which was which. So he weighed his options and chose a different tactic. Dex went up onto his elbow and leaned in, giving Colt time to reject him while analyzing Colt's every reaction. Whereas Wren had always looked like he might bolt if given too much affection, Colt looked starved for attention. Dex was good at indulging people. As their lips met, he felt Colt's breath catch. That one tiny sensation sealed Colt's fate. No matter how many angry words fell from Colt's lips, so too had that needy breath.

"Let me take you to dinner," Dex said before sucking Colt's bottom lip between his teeth. He nibbled. Dex wanted to tease Colt into letting him have his way.

Colt cupped his face, holding him in place and

taking control. He deepened their kiss. Their tongues met and stroked. Dex found himself crawling closer until he straddled Colt's body. He had known Colt would feel amazing beneath him. He kissed like he longed for Dex. It was engrossing. Dex didn't want it to stop. His lips moved to Colt's jaw. He licked and kissed, tasting Colt's neck as he pushed the man's shirt up. The moment he had Colt's shirt high enough, Dex slithered lower and closed his lips around Colt's nipple. Colt's body contracted like he could barely withstand the pleasure. With Colt's every reaction, Dex's hunger built. He kissed his way down Colt's body.

Colt sucked in a hiss as Dex dragged his tongue down the center of his torso. "Isn't the cleaning lady still here? She can probably see us."

She could definitely see them, but Dex felt the way Colt's dick jumped as he made the claim. No matter what he said, he liked the idea of being watched, and Dex didn't have the patience to wait. He had been watching Colt too long. Dex needed to know what sounds he made when he came.

He popped the button on Colt's jeans loose and slowly slid down his zipper. "Are you shy? Or do you relish an audience?" Dex didn't give Colt time to answer before setting his erection free, slithering down his body, and swallowing Colt's cock. Colt's hips left the ground, chasing Dex's mouth.

"Holy shit. Oh my god."

Dex didn't hold back. He sucked and licked. Not only was Dex a master at giving blow jobs, he fucking loved it, and it showed. Dex loved the sounds men made. The way they tasted. More than anything, Dex loved the power he had over a man when their cock hit the back of his throat. Dex knew —in that moment—he truly owned Colt. Colt would do anything, say anything to keep Dex from stopping. He felt Colt's body tense. Dex squeezed, cutting off Colt's orgasm before it hit. Colt's body shook beneath him. Cries assaulted his ears. Dex fought the possessiveness growing inside him as he lightly licked Colt's crown. He could practically feel Colt's insanity. Colt's body relaxed and Dex lightened his hold and went back to work, setting a rhythm meant to please. He knew when he finally let Colt come, his orgasm would rob him of sight in its power. Colt's body tensed again. Dex double his efforts soaking Colt's dick in saliva while he let Colt fuck his mouth. His body burned with need, but this wasn't about him. Colt pulled Dex's hair so hard, his scalp stung as he abused Dex's throat. A loud cry tore from Colt. Hot cum filled Dex's mouth. Dex fought to swallow as much as he could while Colt still pumped inside his mouth.

Colt melted beneath him. "Jesus. Wow. That was... wow. That's never happened to me. I don't mean getting blown. Obviously, that's happened, but goddamn. I think I just had more than one orgasm at once and that's insane. Holy shit."

After a final lick, Dex crawled back up Colt's body and captured his mouth, cutting off the rambling. He would keep Colt happy. Dex was an overachiever in all things. Maybe Dex didn't have a winning personality and he had a lot of quirks that would probably make Colt crazy, but Colt would be happy. He would see.

COLT'S MIND WAS A MESS. ONE SECOND, HE HAD been enjoying the shade and listening to the sounds of nature. The next, his dick had been in Dex's mouth and Dex's talent went beyond description. There was no way he could have predicted Dex would be like this. Obviously, Colt had been fighting an attraction to the guy for a while now, but he hadn't gone as far as fantasizing. If he had, Colt still wouldn't have guessed that Dex was hiding all the blow job know-how the universe had to offer. Jesus, if Wren had given this man up for Haven, what was Haven like? Goddamn. Colt still couldn't breathe. He was like ninety-eight percent certain he had just experienced the fabled multiple orgasm. Colt wanted to try again to be sure.

Dex fixed his clothes and Colt took it because he had lost the ability to properly function. A haze covered his brain and Colt wanted more. Oddly, Dex looked unmoved. He wasn't unkempt or trying for reciprocation. In fact, once Dex set Colt's clothes back to rights, he sat at Colt's side as if waiting for Colt to get his shit together so they could go eat.

"Um." His brain wouldn't work no matter how hard he tried.

Dex's eyebrows rose, silently asking Colt to finish his thoughts.

A burble of uncontrollable laughter rose in Colt's throat. It was a combination of delayed embarrassment and happiness spewing from Colt in the only outlet available to him. A sweet smile curved Dex's lips. There was a hint of sadness to it. The flush on his cheeks made his grayish-blue eyes seem even bluer than usual, making the unhappiness in him show so much clearer than Colt had ever noticed before. He didn't even look directly at Colt—

like Dex knew he wasn't hiding his feelings well. The laughter died on Colt's lips. Emotion punched him in the chest. For the first time, Colt realized Dex was a living, breathing human being with thoughts and feelings. He wasn't just the legendary TV show creator with purse strings that people chased or the cold-hearted playboy billionaire he portrayed. Dex was real and he had rescued Colt. There was no way Dex understood the hell in which he had saved Colt from enduring for another day. Before Colt realized what he would do, he rolled upward into a sitting position and captured Dex's lips. He tasted like cum and hope. It had been so goddamn long since Colt had hope that he almost didn't recognize the sensation overcoming him. For five years, Colt had worked his ass off for Crooked Creek, repaying an old debt to Clint. One Clint had helped create. He had paid in sweat and sex. The shame was deep, but he had fallen far during his addicted years. Colt had allowed Clint to keep him a secret. He had let his life get away from him. While Colt had soaked up the sun, what he had really been soaking up was freedom. Until Dex looked at him with desire, sadness, and zero expectations, Colt hadn't truly recognized the depth of his gratitude. The vastness of Dex's gift.

Colt sucked and nipped at Dex's lips, savoring their kiss. He didn't want it to end. "Tell me how to make you smile and mean it," Colt asked between kisses. He needed to find a way to give the man who had everything something no one else gave.

Dex pulled away but held on to Colt's face. "Why would I smile if I don't mean it?"

Colt never knew what to make of Dex. He had a straightforwardness Colt appreciated. Colt would be the same. "I don't know how to make someone happy who already has everything. There's nothing I can do for you that you can't buy."

"People always lie to me," Dex said unexpectedly. Colt didn't know how to react. Dex kept talking, saving Colt from having to come up with something to say. "Wren doesn't. That why he's my best friend. He's the only person I've ever met who means everything he says. Until I met you, that is. Maybe almost everything you say to me is in anger, but you're honest. There are no undertones when you speak. You don't make me wade my way through our conversations trying to figure out what you really mean versus what you say. I can't buy that."

But he had, and suddenly, Colt didn't like that about himself. He hadn't done much in his life to make himself or anyone else proud. He shifted closer and dragged Dex into his hold, settling Dex into his lap and against his chest so he could enjoy a few more minutes of connection. "The show ends in three days. What amazing creation is up next? I know you haven't been idle."

Thankfully, Dex accepted his topic change. He fell into an explanation of his plans for moving next season to a campsite where contestants would have to fish, hunt, and forage for food on top of doing challenges. This time, if they won, they would have to choose between being safe at voting time or a night at a hotel with dinner provided. Colt hung on every word while silently making some life choices. It was time to decide once and for all how he planned to be a better version of himself when this was done. Dex wasn't like Clint. He wouldn't hide Colt nor would he be interested in keeping him forever. Considering how much Dex had done for Wren, expecting nothing in return, Colt didn't believe Dex would keep him indebted for very long at all. Eventually, Colt would have to become something other than a recovering alcoholic with no future. Accepting Dex's money would be the last time Colt was selfish. He had to change.

"Speaking of the finale, I know you don't want to

take part, but you've been a huge piece of the show's success. You should join me and steal some spotlight. When this is over, you're likely to get acting and modeling offers from all over the world. I understand if you don't want to go back to the ranch, or if you want to pretend you're not with me while you're there or whatever."

Did he want to go? No, but he had just decided to be better. Plus, he couldn't have Dex thinking he was ashamed to be seen with him. The only shame was what Colt had let Clint do to his life. "I'll go. This is important to you. I don't care anything about acting or modeling, but it would probably raise some eyebrows and get people talking if I wasn't there. I don't want anyone talking about anything but your amazing creation."

"That's funny." Dex sounded the exact opposite of his claim. He sounded thoughtful and serious. "I didn't think you considered my creation anything but a plague upon your life."

A snort escaped Colt. He couldn't stop it. "It's been that too, but I'm not blind. I recognize you put something together that became a sensation. Just as you knew it would be. I see the genius in that. At the end of the day, my feelings and I don't matter that much."

Dex moved out of his hold. He twisted, sitting cross-legged across from Colt. "Do you say that because you believe it? Or have you simply accepted it as the truth because other people have always treated you that way?"

Because Dex looked so serious, Colt gave his question the thought it deserved, until his mind wandered and a different thought hit. Dex was always serious. If Colt thought about it, he didn't see Dex smile often. Even when Colt raged in Dex's face over the interruption to his work on the ranch, Dex had been calm and unmoved. Since Dex was still waiting for an answer, Colt shrugged. "I don't know. It just is the truth, I suppose. Why don't you smile very often?"

At his question, Dex's lips quirked—like he had to prove Colt wrong. "Why are you dodging my question? Did I make you uncomfortable with dismissing yourself as unimportant?"

A smile exploded across Colt's face. Their conversations always turned out odd. Dex had gone from blowing Colt's mind to picking at his brain, and that was what it was always like with him. One extreme to another. He enraged Colt and turned him on, but Colt also genuinely believed Dex cared more about people than anyone realized. It was just hidden behind his strange and abrasive personality. Colt liked talking to him more than he wanted to admit.

"Maybe it's both," he said, answering Dex's earlier question. "I believe I'm unimportant and other people have shown me it's true. But I also don't wallow in my lot, because it's just part of life. Most people aren't that special. We're all just cogs, keeping the world moving. When we're gone, more cogs will take our place. Eventually, no one will remember us at all. Well, the world will probably always remember you, but I'll be forgotten in months... if that long. The least I can do is go with you to your season finale and be closer to someone who will go down in history than most people ever get. That's something."

Dex looked as if he had turned inside himself. His gaze never quite met Colt's. When he spoke, he sounded distant, yet every word struck a chord with Colt. "If I go down in history, I hope it's because—even after I'm gone—people are finding an escape while watching my shows. I want them to tune out whatever horrible thing they're facing in real life for an hour and disappear inside what I made for them. That's all I'm trying to do."

Colt was mesmerized by Dex. In that moment,

he saw real magic and it was blinding. Inside Dex, there was a passion for something beyond what most people ever felt, and he had shown Colt a glimpse of it. Like that, Colt just wanted to be with him, even if they were never more than they were right then. For the first time in Colt's life, he was completely awestruck by someone. He wanted more.

FIVE

WAITING for the final live show to begin was murder. Dex was busy and Colt was just hanging out at the fringes of the area set up for the night's events. Cast and crew were milling around, talking and doing various jobs. Someone had set up chairs for them before their arrival and that was where Dex had left him. Colt spaced out, waiting for things to get moving. The sooner this was over, the faster he would be alone with Dex again. It was almost funny how quickly he had gotten addicted to having Dex to himself. Then again, Colt was an addict all the way to his greedy soul.

"Dude, you know you could have just told me you're gay and I would've stopped trying to hook up with you."

Colt eyebrows snapped together. His hackles immediately rose at just the sound of Becca's voice as she appeared over his shoulder. He tried smoothing out his features as she moved to stand next to him. It was no longer his responsibility to pick up her slack. He could let some things go. "Why would I bring up my sexuality at work?"

She looked thoughtful for a moment. "I guess I could see that. It was easy for me to forget you were actually working. I was just trying to win a lot of money and have as much fun as possible in the process," she added with a laugh. "Still, it's awesome about Dex and you. He still doesn't smile, but I can tell he's happy. And damn, dude, you look a hell of a lot more relaxed."

"You might still win that money." He didn't want to talk about Dex with Becca. Colt couldn't explain it. Being with Dex was something for him and him alone.

A bright smile lit Becca's face. She fluffed her dark curls. "We'll see." With that hanging in the air, Becca flounced off to flirt with some guys who worked in lighting. Colt shook his head. He supposed he had been young and flirtatious once. When he had met Wren, Colt had found himself flirting again for the first time in ages. Ninety-eight percent of the time, Colt didn't feel that carefree. He could see why Dex wanted Wren around. It was nice to bask in the glow of youth. Colt had tossed those years away on a dream he never achieved. Jesus. He needed to get out of this place. Being at Crooked Creek reminded him too much of all the mistakes he had made. They were many.

The hair on the back of Colt's neck stood as Clint stepped outside. The bright lights meant for the outdoor stage highlighted all his harsh features. He was big and strawberry blonde. Even the scruff covering the lower half of his face had hints of red smattered throughout. His eyes were a gorgeous shade of amber that Colt had never seen on anyone else. Up close, there was no missing the light freckles on his nose and cheeks. The first time Clint smiled at Colt, Colt had been a goner. There had been so much hunger in Clint's expression as he had checked Colt out on the sly. When Clint had given in to temptation that first time, Colt had felt like the most irresistible man on the planet. He was the reason Clint had stepped across a line Clint had never dared cross before. It hadn't taken long for reality to strike its blow, though. Colt was a secret. Not only had he been nothing to Clint publicly, Clint had schemed and plotted to ensure Colt would be trapped in his hidden web. Clint was also the reason Colt had started drinking heavily. Everything about falling in love with Clint had broken Colt until Colt felt nothing but hatred. As he watched Clint close the distance between them, Colt fought the urge to run. Fear hit from nowhere, side-swiping Colt. Clint had found a way to own Colt once already. He could do it again. Colt could never, ever go back to that life.

Clint shoved his hands in his pockets as he came to stand over Colt. Even while sitting in one of Dex's director-style chairs, Colt had to tilt his chin up to meet Clint's stare. Clint didn't speak. He simply held Colt's gaze with the same hunger he had the night they met.

Colt couldn't take the pressure. "What?"

A muscle jumped in Clint's jaw at Colt's impatient-sounding question. "You've been ignoring my calls and texts."

"Actually, I blocked your number."

Irritation flashed in Clint's eyes, but he obviously realized he was no longer in control. "Just tell me what you need to come back."

It was odd. Even just six months ago, Colt would have killed to hear those words from Clint. He had silently pled for ages for any sign of hope for them or even just an opportunity to say he wanted to matter to Clint. Now there was nothing but this deep well of resentment sitting in Colt's gut. He didn't even know where to start saying all the things he had been forced to keep to himself. Colt had to say something, or he would never forgive himself.

"It's too late, but even if it wasn't, we both know you never would have given me what I needed to stay."

Clint's eyes hardened and Colt braced himself against whatever cruel words would follow. Before they fell, Dex materialized at his side like magic. He pressed his lips to Colt's temple as he slipped into the chair beside him. "Hello, sexy cowboy. What have I missed?"

It was such a small thing, but Dex's greeting was exactly what Colt needed at the exact moment he needed it. His open claiming of Colt was everything Clint had denied Colt. It was a breath of fresh air when he had been drowning for so many years.

Colt's gaze slid Dex's way. He hoped the man saw how much Colt appreciated him. "Clint was telling me how poorly this place is doing without me. He was trying to lure me back."

Irritation flashed in Dex's eyes as he focused on Clint. "I'm sure I've already told you that Colt is off limits now." He set his hand on Colt's knee. "Even if

Colt needed to work, which he doesn't, my schedule is too full to accommodate a working spouse. Plus, it's just poor taste for someone with my money to allow their husband to work."

It took every ounce of Colt's considerable will to stop him from looking Dex's way in horror. He was ninety-five percent certain the words were only a dig at Clint, but still. Colt's horror slipped away, replaced with a deep satisfaction at Clint's expression. He was devastated. Maybe Colt's reaction to seeing Clint's pain made him a bad person, but no one knew how much he had earned this moment.

"You're getting married." It wasn't a question, but Colt still treated Clint's remark as one.

"Yes."

Clint's chest expanded. Then, to Colt's surprise, he walked away without comment.

Dex squeezed Colt's knee, reminding Colt he hadn't moved his hand. "Don't worry, gorgeous. We'll have a long engagement so you can adjust yourself to the idea."

Colt's head whipped around, nearly giving him whiplash. "What?"

Dex looked unfazed by Colt's panicked tone. He stared back at Colt like a man who never heard no. "I believe we've already established that I'm a man of my word. Clint will tell people and I can't have anyone thinking I'm a liar or would back out of an engagement. Plus, I like you better than anyone else."

Colt blinked. Dex said the words as if everyone married for that reason. "That's the craziest thing I've ever heard."

Dex shook his head. "Actually, insanity is doing the same thing repeatedly while expecting different results. I, on the other hand, always learn from my mistakes. When I liked Wren better than anyone else, I didn't act upon it and he got away. I plan to do things differently with you. You let Clint buy you and destroy you. Do you really want to do the same thing with me, or would you like to try something different?"

Fuck. That actually sounded reasonable, which kind of fucked with Colt a little. Yet, a wave of sadness washed over him. There was no dreaming or romance in his life. There never had been. Until now, he hadn't realized how much he had secretly hoped for those things. Then, the strangest moment of his life became even weirder. He swore Dex read his mind.

Dex leaned over and pressed his lips to Colt's,

stealing all the oxygen from him. His lips parted as Dex sucked lightly on his bottom lip. Dex enthralled him to the point he forgot where he was for a moment, and how many people were watching.

"It's okay, angel," Dex whispered against his lips. "I know I'm not who you want."

It was like getting punched in the throat. Not only was Dex who he wanted, Colt fucking hated the hurt in Dex's words. Dex had rescued him and that was romantic as hell. Colt gently held Dex's face so he couldn't get away. He deepened their kiss, pouring his feelings into every stroke of his tongue. It had been so long since Colt was free to do as he pleased. He had forgotten he could be the one in charge of his happiness. Colt pulled away, but he didn't let Dex go.

He kept his voice low, ensuring their conversation remained private as he held Dex's stare. Colt wanted him to see the honesty in his eyes. "You are who I want. Don't say that to me again." He didn't need someone else to give him romance. Colt could be the one who provided it. In fact, Colt felt more empowered than he ever had in his life as Dex stared at him with his heart in his eyes. He would bet money no one else had ever made Dex Wise look the way he did now—like Colt had something to offer

Dex that he didn't already own. Colt brushed his lips across Dex's one more time. "Go do your thing so we can go home." A smile that felt wicked even to Colt pulled at his lips. "You've got work to do there too."

Dex gave him a subtle nod. "You're right. I do." He stole another quick kiss from Colt. "And I'm way more excited about that job than this one at the moment." He winked before pushing from the chair and leaving Colt behind. It took Colt a minute to realize everyone was staring at him. He fought the satisfied smile trying to burst free. It had been so long since he had what he wanted that Colt sometimes had a hard time recognizing Dex gave him everything. Right now, though, with all heads turned their way and jealous glances being tossed in his direction, Colt saw the truth. He really did have a life they should envy. Dex was amazing. Colt wouldn't forget it again.

ONCE COLT PUT THE IDEA OF GOING HOME IN Dex's head, the rest of the night crawled. By the time they pulled into the garage, Dex was ready to tear off his skin. Colt's silence didn't help. Dex was having one of his off nights. He was barely stopping himself from rocking himself in the corner. Everything had been too loud. Clint's hatred glared at Dex every time he turned around. Becca had won and her screams had nearly taken out his eardrums. Dex's shirt, which was richly made in one of the few materials he could stand against his skin, was squeezing the life from him. He needed distraction before an episode hit. His hands shook as he put the car in park. Then Colt was there—as if he felt Dex's desperation.

Their tongues met and stroked. His shirt loosened, making Dex realize Colt unbuttoned it. Relief washed over Dex as his mind went quiet. He wasn't ready to fall apart in front of Colt yet. Not to mention, Colt had been so damn hot at the ranch earlier, Dex didn't want to ruin their night. Colt's kiss was amazing. Every single time he kissed Dex, Colt came at him like he was beyond turned on. It was sexy and empowering. Dex never doubted it was him Colt wanted. Not his money or anything else Dex could give him. Just him.

"I want to see you come," Colt growled between kisses. "You haven't come for me yet. I want it."

Dex was so turned on, his brain itched with want. He had been craving Colt since the first time he saw him. Colt was the first time in Dex's life he hadn't immediately acted upon his desires. Instead, he had waited, gauged the best way to own him, and been methodical in his plan. Even now that he could have him, Dex still worked at making himself equally as necessary to Colt as Colt was to Dex.

"Get inside."

Colt gripped Dex's jaw and held him in place for a punishing kiss. Dex's body burned. Every thought in his head disappeared. Colt bit his bottom lip before pulling away and holding his stare. Madness flashed in Colt's eyes. "No. Come for me. I like to watch. Pull out your dick and come for me. We're not moving until you do. You like to slip away before I can hear you moan."

That was true, but Dex had his reasons for backing off before Colt could pleasure him. Dex could concede this one thing. His skin felt too tight as he shifted positions and undid his button. Dex didn't think Colt had been exaggerating about liking to watch. His hungry gaze ate up every move Dex made. It had been a long time since anyone made him feel as sexy as Colt did. If Dex knew nothing else about Colt, he knew Colt wanted him sexually. Maybe Colt could walk away from everything else Dex had to offer, but he wouldn't walk away from this. Not yet.

The fact that Colt kept kissing him and didn't try staring at him directly made it easy for Dex to slide down his zipper. As long as Colt let Dex move at his pace and didn't try to take charge, Dex would be fine. He closed his mind to those thoughts and set his erection free. Colt made a humming noise that blanked Dex's mind. He honestly couldn't recall a time he had been this aroused. Because Colt was important to him, Dex wanted a full life with him. Colt wasn't a forgotten name in the dark where Dex took his pleasure in the only way he could before walking away without another thought. Dex would see Colt after this. They would have breakfast across from each other and sleep in the same bed at night. Those things meant Dex needed to find a level of normalcy with Colt. There needed to be comfort in an uncomfortable act. The only way Dex could achieve that was by being completely in control.

"If you want me to moan, then wrap your fingers around my dick."

Colt kept his gaze locked on Dex's lap. It was sexy as hell—like Colt was enthralled. Colt proved he could follow instructions without complaint as his fingers wrapped around Dex's cock. Dex fought a shuddered breath. Colt's palm was hot. His grip was tight.

"Stroke me, gorgeous cowboy. Make me come."

Dex nibbled Colt's ear to keep the man from looking his way. Not only did Dex not like being focused on directly, he really didn't like it when someone watched him while they were touching his dick. The two things combined were too intimate. That made his insides squirm uncomfortably. Colt's touch was amazing. He kept his strokes steady. Dex's breathing turned ragged against the shell of Colt's ear.

Whispered words escaped him as his hips lifted, seeking more. "That's it. Harder." Colt's hold tightened. A gasp escaped Dex. "Faster." Even Dex heard the desperation in his voice as his body tensed. Colt's motions quickened. "Yes. Goddamn. Just like that. Don't stop." Dex held Colt's face as he sucked the man's ear and neck, fighting the urge to bite. Biting was a huge release of stress for him, but he had forced himself to break that habit a long time ago when he had gotten really bad about it. In fact, he rarely wore short sleeves, even in the Texas heat, because bite marks scarred his skin. The struggle was real at the moment. Then, the dam broke. A wave of ecstasy washed over Dex. He rocked upward, riding Colt's palm as the man massaged out every drop of cum. Colt turned his head and captured Dex's mouth, swallowing the sounds Dex couldn't control. Every strange and overwhelming impulse Dex experienced in an out-of-control moment faded beneath Colt's soul-consuming kiss. Dex couldn't focus on anything else other than the pleasure Colt dragged from him. His impromptu move of announcing their marriage earlier felt more than right in that moment. Being incapable of controlling his whims usually caused him trouble, but not in this instance. Colt brought out something good inside Dex. Their life together would always mirror that happiness. Tonight, though, Dex needed to make Colt scream.

CUM COVERED COLT'S SHIRT. HE PEELED IT UP and over his head as he headed for the back door. He swore he could feel Dex at his back, stalking him like prey. His body burned. Dex had been so demanding and controlling. Sex with him would be rough and practiced. Arousal owned Colt. He was beyond ready to have Dex make him scream. All night, Dex's gaze had moved his way. Promise had tinted every heated glance. Now Colt needed Dex to make good on the silent threats his eyes made.

Colt didn't make it inside. His chest hit the door as Dex overcame him, shoving him against the solid piece. Colt clung to the cool wood as Dex tore at his jeans. He tried digging his fingernails into the door, scratching for purchase as Dex's teeth sank into his ass cheek the moment it was bare. Dex sucked as he bit, bringing the blood to the surface and making Colt's eyes roll back in his head.

"Don't move," Dex growled as he peeled away the bottom half of Colt's clothes. Colt didn't dare disobey. He was scared Dex would stop if he did. Dex nipped at his ass again, placing biting kisses on both cheeks. By the time he roughly grabbed Colt's balls, his cry was louder than he expected. It reverberated from the walls of the garage, assaulting his ears.

"That's right," Dex said, biting Colt's shoulder. "Who owns this dick?" He squeezed and pulled, weakening Colt's knees.

"You do." His voice shook. Colt bit his lip, trying to stop his neediness from spilling out. Being with Clint hadn't been this way. With Clint, Colt had been a ready hole to fuck. Colt's pleasure hadn't mattered at all. With Dex, it was like Colt's pleasure was all that mattered.

Dex swiped the side of his hand down Colt's

crack until he roughly fingered his asshole. "Who owns this asshole?" Dex asked as he immediately went for the prostate.

Colt turned desperate in an instant. "You do." Jesus, even he heard the whiney begging in his voice. He was the whore, pleading to get fucked. Dex was ruining him a little more for everyone else with every encounter.

"You will paint my back door with your cum, marking this place as yours, because I fucking said so, understood?"

Colt pressed his forehead to the door, squeezed his eyes shut, and nodded. He was so close. So fucking close.

Dex's grip turned painful. "Is that understood?"

"Yes."

"Good boy," Dex whispered. The pumping on Colt's cock sped. Dex's fingers moved inside his ass, destroying Colt's mind. Colt shamelessly squirmed, seeking more.

"Please? Oh god. Please?" Without warning, Colt's entire body seized. He didn't care at all that he begged. Ecstasy crashed over him, making him shake as Dex shook Colt's cum out, painting the door just as he warned. All Colt could do was open-mouthed gasp against the wood while wave after wave rocked him to his core.

A sweet, light kiss brushed his shoulder followed by the lightest lick. Dex's touch softened, becoming a caress. "You're so beautiful. So perfect. I'll always take care of you. You'll see."

Colt believed. In that moment, Colt was more certain of Dex than he had ever been of anything or anyone in his life. If Dex claimed he was secretly a king right then, Colt would have taken it as gospel. Everything about Dex was obviously magic. Colt prayed hard in that moment that he would never stop being the center of Dex's focus. He couldn't lose this feeling Dex gave him. Goddamn. He thought there was a very real chance he was falling in love. Fuck him. Colt hadn't seen that one coming.

SIX

AFTER TURNING ALL the dry goods and canned goods label out in the cabinets, rearranging the fridge, and making sure everything was either symmetrical or lined up from tallest to shortest in the kitchen, Dex had no other choice but to sit down. He spent several minutes trying to get the flower centerpiece in the actual center of the table before forcing himself to let it go. Colt's coffee cup was still full, but Dex imagined it was cold. His breakfast had barely been touched. Dex openly stared at him. In nothing but workout shorts, Colt was mesmerizing. His hands were darker than the rest of his body, but not by much. That meant Dex had obviously been missing out on Colt being shirtless around the ranch. Everything about Colt was perfectly balanced. That made the perfectionist inside Dex purr. His sexy blue gaze was locked on something across the room and he didn't blink. Dex knew that spaced out look. Colt was here in body, but his mind had gone somewhere only he could see. Dex was beyond curious to know Colt's thoughts. Sometimes, Dex felt like he knew Colt. Other times, he recognized he didn't know Colt at all.

"Where are you at right now?"

Colt blinked, as if returning to earth. His gaze focused on Dex. A sheepish smile tugged at his lips. "Sorry."

"Don't apologize. I'm the same way when I'm plotting a new show. You'll see. What were you creating?"

A slight blush touched Colt's cheeks. He stood and carried his plate to the sink. Colt froze halfway there and looked around the kitchen. "Wow. I never realized you're this OCD." He set his plate inside the sink. "I'll try to do better."

Dex blinked at the comment. "What's that supposed to mean?"

Colt carelessly waved toward the open-faced cabinets. "Next time I get groceries, I'll try to remember you like things perfect."

For a moment, Dex tried to decide how to

respond. He wasn't ready to show Colt any weakness, but he also didn't know how to set Colt at ease. Wren had told him to use his words. Dex wasn't good at that. He tried. "Don't worry about that. I was just giving my hands something to do while you worked out whatever you're plotting. Which I haven't forgotten about, by the way."

"What sort of madman gets up at seven a.m. every day when he doesn't have to?" Colt asked, still dodging.

Dex fought a growl. He didn't want to talk about his need to set an alarm for the same time every morning no matter where he slept. Dex had quirks. Colt was trying him with this avoidance. "I do. Self-discipline is very important to me. Stop stalling."

Colt's chest expanded as he took a deep breath, fascinating Dex. "Don't laugh." That comment had Dex's gaze snapping back to Colt's as he moved back to sit at the table.

"I'm certain I've never laughed at you. So I don't know why you think I would now."

He looked uncomfortable as hell, which made Dex's curiosity double. "Well, because it's dumb, so I can't really blame you if you laugh, but you asked, so." Colt shrugged, obviously trying to delay the inevitable. Before Dex could demand he speak, Colt let it fly. "I came up with a concept for a video game." His blush deepened. Dex couldn't look away. He also couldn't figure out why Colt was so embarrassed, but that was pretty normal for Dex. He didn't understand most people or their reactions.

"Okay."

Colt tried backpedaling. "Really, I just had a dream and it won't leave me alone. Like two years ago, I had a day off and I spent the whole day playing video games. That night, I had this weird dream where I was stuck in the digital world—like I was the player. I spent the whole night trying to magic this fox I was chasing into a new realm."

"Like an actual fox? The animal," Dex said, clarifying his question. The way Colt blushed made Dex realize his question made things worse, but truly he was only trying to get a mental image of Colt's dream.

Colt nodded. "The animal. I was being chased by a bear the whole time," he added, as if that explained everything. "Anyhow, when I woke up, this dream stuck with me and I started thinking about all the tiny details. Why was the bear chasing me? Why did I need to save the fox and use magic to send it elsewhere? With every question I asked, the bigger the story grew. So, for the past two years, I've been working it out in my head. I have like eight pretty extensive levels planned out." His gaze slid away, as if he had revealed too much to Dex. "It's just a way I entertain myself, I guess. My escape."

That last bit punched Dex in the chest. He had done the same, creating worlds in his mind to get away from reality. To survive being different. Dex stood. "Is the bear and the fox the first level?"

Colt nodded. "It's the most simplistic."

Dex motioned for Colt to follow, asking more questions as they headed down the hall. "Do you think you can paint me a picture and describe how you would beat each level?"

"Yes." Colt sounded unsure, but he didn't back down.

Dex led Colt into his office. He motioned for Colt to sit while he grabbed his sketch pad. He paced as he drew a bear and a fox. Nothing too detailed. Just a simple likeness. Dex always worked better when his feet were moving. "Okay. Tell me everything." Dex paced and nodded along as Colt walked him through everything. He sketched and made notes, ripping out pages as they filled. Dex lined them up on the floor, creating a pattern. His room to pace disappeared as they created a new world at their feet. When he was done, Dex stared at the picture on the floor, letting it come together in his mind. He nodded. "This is good. You have a lot of natural talent. I'll give Lynx Hirata a call. He's a game designer. I'm certain he would love this."

"Wait." Colt sounded confused. "Are you being serious?"

Dex focused on Colt. He looked uncomfortable. "Of course. Everyone knows I'm a master at spotting talent and knowing what will sell in today's market. This could be huge for you."

Colt stared at the drawings on the floor. "But this is just a stupid dream."

"Dreams aren't stupid. They're a manifestation of our creative talents. Not everyone taps into it, but you have. This is really good, Colt. This is what you were meant to do."

"I don't know what to say." Colt's eyes were soft as he stared up at Dex—like he cared about Dex. It was too hard to resist.

Dex closed the distance between them until he stood over Colt. "Say you'll let me handle the negotiations so you get the best deal, and I promise I'll make sure your dream is treated with the respect it deserves."

"Why would you do this for me?" Colt's voice shook, confusing Dex. "I don't mean just the game.

Why are you doing any of this for me? Nothing is free. No one is nice to me for no reason and the price is always higher than I can pay. So, why?"

"We're getting married. Why wouldn't I do everything I can for you?" Dex didn't understand why Colt thought things were complicated. They weren't. Colt had talent. Dex knew the right people.

Colt still didn't look mollified. "That's what everyone will think too. They'll think I didn't earn this. That you bought it for me."

Confusion had Dex's forehead furrowing. "I don't understand why you care what people think. There will never come a day when everyone feels the same way about anything at all. All anyone cares about is their opinion. They think, if they hate something someone else creates, then that person must not have talent. If they're jealous or bitter, they honestly believe that invalidates the creator somehow. That's not true. Just like it doesn't matter how your dream becomes reality. It would never happen if you hadn't had the dream to begin with. People's opinions only have as much power as you give them." Dex waved toward the papers on the floor. "You did this. This is yours. I can't call Lynx about an idea that doesn't exist, and it wouldn't without you. It's okay to be proud of yourself. I think you're amazing."

Colt slowly came to his feet. His gaze never wavered from Dex. As usual, Dex couldn't get a read on Colt. As Colt lowered his head, Dex automatically met him halfway. Maybe Dex couldn't always understand how other people thought, but his body knew Colt owned him and always went with Colt while Dex's mind caught up. This kiss was different from any other kiss they had shared. It was sweet. Colt lightly held Dex's hips while barely capturing Dex's bottom lip between his. There was a tugging in Dex's chest. No one had ever made him feel the way he currently felt. New things weren't necessarily good things to Dex. He needed time to adjust. While he felt good, Dex also felt off balance. The only thing stopping Dex from jumping away was the fact that Colt didn't try for anything else. He kept his kiss light. There were no expectations. For a moment, they were connected, and it was... nice. The urge to give Colt more than anyone else ever had doubled. He stepped back.

"Let's go shopping."

Colt's expression blanked. "Right now?"

Dex gave him a sharp nod. "You need a new computer to keep track of these ideas. Plus, I want to add you to my wireless plan and get you a better phone. Really, there are a thousand things we need to do." Because Colt was his and Dex would ensure he was cared for in every way.

"Don't you have work to do today?" Colt asked while shifting from foot to foot.

Dex gathered the sketches, making sure they stayed in order. "This is more important." Not to mention, people worked around his schedule. Not the other way around. Dex needed to make Colt happy right now. His heart demanded it. Logically, Dex recognized that financial security and the opportunity to further his dreams were the only things Dex had to offer. That was all he brought to the table. Colt was nice, sexy, hardworking, and normal. He could have anyone he chose. Colt had chosen Dex. Dex needed to do everything within his power to ensure that Colt never regretted his decision, because god knew, Dex would test him. That much was inevitable.

THE URGE TO CHEW HIS FINGERNAILS WAS crippling. Even though Dex had assured him that Lynx loved Colt's video game idea, meeting Lynx for lunch was a whole new level of soul exposure Colt was unaccustomed to handling. Dex had years of experience with having his work criticized and rejected. Colt hadn't even wanted to tell Dex about his idea, much less a famous game designer. This was hell. Colt damn near begged Dex to come with him to this meeting. Dex had booted him from the house alone. He had assured Colt that Colt would be great. Colt didn't feel great. He felt sick. The restaurant Lynx had chosen made Colt grateful Dex had bought him a fuck ton of new clothes. Otherwise, he never would have been allowed through the door. Like all the stores Dex had taken him to, there were no prices on the menu. No doubt he would die when the bill came. Colt was out of ways to distract himself from his nerves.

"Colt?"

Colt came to his feet with his hand held out as the man appeared at the edge of his table. No doubt he looked as jumpy as he felt. Lynx was the opposite of the restaurant. In fact, he looked so out of place that Colt's brain experienced a hard reset and he didn't hear Lynx's first words. Colt reclaimed his seat as Lynx moved to sit across from him. His multi-colored hair was spiked into a short Mohawk and his vintage-looking gamer t-shirt had a rip at the collar.

There was a small diamond in Lynx's nose. All of those details paled in comparison to Lynx's light green eyes. They were at such odds with his obvious Asian descent that Colt was completely speechless for a full minute.

Lynx didn't seem to notice. He moved his menu out of his way and propped his elbows on the table before focusing his full attention on Colt. "You are every bit the sexy cowboy Dex described."

To Colt's horror, a blush crept up his face. "I'm not wearing my barn clothes today, so I don't know what gives me away as a cowboy."

"Ah," Lynx said, dragging out the word and showing some flair. "But you can't hide from your roots. You're tan in a pale world and have that hot accent. Some things you can't escape. Just look at me." He motioned down his body. "My dad owns the biggest tech company in the entire United States. And yes, I am his biggest disappointment. I decided if I was meant to be the black sheep no matter how I tried, then I would be the most fabulous black sheep you've ever seen. Of course, this drove my father insane, until I turned his most hated of my hobbies into a multi-million-dollar company. So, you see, you can't escape your roots."

"May I take your order?"

Lynx's odd-colored gaze swung the waiter's way at the man's interruption. "You know I never actually eat here, Jeeves. The food is terrible, but I will have your cheapest and most American beer. Please and thank you." Colt bit the inside of his cheek to keep from laughing as Lynx shooed the man away. He was a good eighty percent sure the guy's name was not Jeeves. Lynx focused on him once more and went back to his story like they hadn't been interrupted. "Anyhow, since I couldn't dodge the tech gene, I decided to change my name and my looks."

"And you went with Lynx?"

Lynx didn't look the least bit offended at Colt's surprise. "Yes, because if you want to work in the video game industry, you have to learn one lesson. There will always be someone faster, stronger, more driven, and hungrier. They'll produce faster than you and get more sales than you. Those people will sell their souls and first born to always be on top, but you have one thing they don't. You have a Lynx on your side. So, I'll have my lawyer email Dex's lawyer the contract. They'll find it to be fair and mutually beneficial because my lawyer is also Dex's lawyer and I'm a fair kind of guy. By the way, congrats on the upcoming nuptials. Dex is a great guy."

Colt blinked. And then he blinked again. He

didn't think Lynx had taken a single breath in that entire spiel. But Colt also didn't think he imagined the fact that Lynx intended to make his game a reality. He didn't get to cheer, because Lynx had taken a breath and was off again.

"Do you want to eat somewhere else? I'm kind of hungry, but I never eat here. Their food is awful and pretentious. I just like making them endure my presence, because I'm too rich to throw out into the street. There's a chicken place down the street with wings and beer. Do you know the place?"

"Yes." Colt barely got his answer out before Lynx talked over him.

"Fantastic." He jumped to his feet and headed for the door before Colt had time to react. He spoke over his shoulder as he walked away. "I'll meet you there." He raised his voice for the entire restaurant to hear. "Jeeves, put my bill on my tab. Give yourself a huge tip. Excellent service as always."

Colt didn't know what had him smiling the hardest: Lynx's over-the-top personality, the fact that he had just witnessed the beginning of his dream coming true, or the bright red boxers with giant white hearts Lynx wore that were hanging out the huge rip in the ass of his jeans for the world to see. Colt shook his head and came to his feet. It seemed they were eating elsewhere. He flashed the waiter a sympathetic smile as he headed out. Colt understood what it was like to be the person on the fringes of the elite's insanity. With his brain still frozen with shock from the Lynx encounter, Colt walked right into someone as he stepped outside.

"Excuse—" The apology died on his lips. Clint stared down at him, taking up too much space and looking like he wouldn't be budged.

"Hey, Colt."

"Hey." Even to his ears, Colt's greeting sounded strained. He had a bad feeling—like Clint had been following him. There was no way this was a coincidence.

"How have you been?"

"Good, and you?" Colt asked without thought. He didn't want to prolong this conversation. Manners were ingrained in him. The response had been automatic.

"I sold the ranch."

"Really?" Damn. Surprise got him that time. He should walk away, but that was rude.

Clint nodded. "You know I've always hated that place. Now, with you gone, it seems pointless to keep trying to keep my father's dream alive. I think I want to do what I want for once."

"Oh." Colt had nothing else. He was uncomfortable. Colt eased toward the curb where his truck sat. "I'm sorry, but I have a business meeting."

"When I get settled in my new place, you should come check it out," Clint said, ignoring Colt's attempt at getting away.

"That's not a good idea."

Clint wasn't deterred. "I'm trying to change."

The claim had Colt seeing red in an instant. His temper snapped. "You're a bit late to the game now, Clint. You literally had years to do things differently. It's not like you didn't know you were killing me."

Clint's eyes fell closed. His chin dropped. As Colt looked on, Clint's wide chest expanded as he dragged in a deep breath before meeting Colt's stare again. "I'm not too late if I'm changing for me."

There was a fuck you on the tip of Colt's tongue, but he didn't let it fall. Instead, he turned away. He couldn't care about being rude. Clint hadn't cared about anything he had done to Colt over the years. No matter what Clint said, it was too late.

"I'm sorry, Colt."

Colt didn't look back as the words slammed into him. There was no way Clint would ever be as sorry as Colt was for the life he had allowed Clint to steal from him. Unexpectedly, as Colt climbed behind the wheel of his truck, a smile tugged at his lips. He had Dex now. Maybe Dex would never love him, but at least he cared. He was good and Colt needed all the goodness he could get after Clint. Dex was fresh air after a life in hell. Clint could show up a million times, claiming he had changed. It didn't matter. Colt had changed too. He no longer believed he wasn't worth more than what Clint had given him. Dex gave him everything money could and couldn't buy. Colt's heart no longer saw anyone else. In fact, he couldn't wait to get back home to Dex.

SEVEN

THEY HAD LOST power overnight for just long enough that Dex's alarm clock didn't go off at seven. That was it. That was the moment his day had gone off the rails. From there, things had slowly spun out of control for Dex. While he was still semi-functioning, there was a tiny warning bell clanging in the back of his head, warning a meltdown was right around the corner. Dex did everything within his power to stave off the attack.

For the hundredth time, Colt looked his way with worry etching his features. "Are you sure you're okay?"

A smile that felt as faked as it was pulled at Dex's lips. "Of course, sexy cowboy. You shouldn't worry so much about me." A loud bang on the TV made Dex jump and cringe on the inside. His smile ratcheted up. He really didn't want to snap.

Colt's expression shifted, turning nervous. "I forgot to tell you. I ran into Clint the other day. While I was at lunch with Lynx," he added, explaining why Dex hadn't known about it.

Dex popped his neck, trying to ease the growing tension. "Was he following you?"

Colt didn't answer right away, putting Dex even more on edge. When Colt spoke, he sounded hesitant. "I'm not sure, but he said he's sold the ranch. So I was thinking, if the show does get renewed next year, you could probably still film there. You know, if the studio demands it or whatever."

Dex gave no fucks about the show right now. He wanted to know why Clint was following his man. "Do I need to get a restraining order against him for you?"

Colt smiled, as if amused by the suggestion. "That's not necessary. Even if he was a threat, which he isn't, I'm more than capable of taking care of myself."

"That's not the point," Dex said, raising his voice more than he liked. "You're mine. He shouldn't be talking to you at all anymore."

A deep line appeared between Colt's eyebrows. He looked understandably confused by Dex's inexplicable anger. "What's going on with you today? You've been twitchy since we got up this morning. Now it's like you want to start a fight and I don't understand why. I mean, I kind of feel like I shouldn't bother telling you things in the future if you plan to lose your shit every time I run into Clint."

Dex tried taking a breath. It didn't help. Still, he tried tempering his voice. It wasn't Colt's fault he didn't know Dex or that Dex was having an off day. "You're always fine to tell me anything. I just don't think for one second that you accidentally ran into Clint. I think Clint accidentally on purpose ran into you. That's definitely borderline stalking, at the very least."

A sexy and wicked-looking smile pulled at Colt's lips. "Are you saying you wouldn't stalk me if someone else stole me away?"

Dex's eye twitched. He inched closer to complete overload. "You sound like you want to be punished."

Colt shrugged, trying and failing to look innocent. "How much can you claim to want me if you would just let me get away without a fight?"

With his mind a squirming mess, Dex needed the release Colt promised with his impish game. "Go to our room and strip." The way Colt immediately stood to obey only made Dex's hunger grow. As Colt headed down the hall, Dex followed at a slower pace. While Colt stripped, Dex tried hard not to stare. Instead, he moved to the bathroom and grabbed a duffle bag from beneath the sink. He barely spared Colt a glance as he set the bag on the nightstand and rolled up his sleeves. "Get in the bed. Arms above your head."

A nervous-sounding chuckle caressed Dex's ears as he dug a pair of Velcro cuffs from the bag. When Dex wove them through the headboard and strapped Colt's hands inside, Colt started to babble. "I've never noticed the scars on your arms. Is that why you always wear long sleeves? What happened?"

Dex ignored the questions. He intentionally kept his arms covered until they were in bed each night. Now wasn't the time to get into it. Dex had plans for Colt. He let his gaze slide down Colt's nude body. Colt was hard and ready. He had a long wait for relief. Dex moved back to the bag. He found a ball gag. Colt's eyes widened. Dex felt his features harden. It was out of his control. "You'll need this," he promised as he slipped it over Colt's head. Dex waited until Colt couldn't respond to say more. "As much as I love hearing you scream and beg, you did practically demand to be punished today. I'm indulging you." And the itching in his brain had eased at the distraction Colt offered.

Dex grabbed the bag and carried it to the bed. He pulled out a short metal rod with ankle cuffs attached and twisted to extend it until it was the perfect length to keep Colt's thighs spread wide for him. Colt didn't struggle as Dex finished strapping him in for his torture, but his eyes looked panicked. Dex couldn't have that. He lightly stroked Colt's cock until he relaxed.

With Colt calm, Dex climbed onto the mattress. He settled between Colt's spread legs and dragged the bag closer. With his gaze locked on Colt's twitching cock, Dex spoke as he worked. "I don't think you looked very hard if you went looking for my toys your first night here. But I wonder if you would have run if you'd found them." He dug out the lube and went to work thoroughly oiling Colt's cock, balls, and asshole. He would need it. With Colt ready for him, Dex pulled a twelve-inch dildo from the bag and oiled it next. Colt looked panicked again. Dex played with Colt's crown until he relaxed once more. "Don't worry. You can take it." He fingered

Dex's asshole, slowly adding more fingers until he was four fingers in, and then he pushed the tip of the dildo inside. He worked it deeper and deeper, mimicking sex until he had Colt filled to capacity. Colt's stomach and chest rose and fell as he fought for air. Dex was transfixed by him.

An evil chuckle fell from Dex's lips as he dug through the bag. "I doubt Clint ever played with you. He probably always bent you over the first piece of furniture he reached in the dark and fucked you barely lubed. You were left to jack off later after he quickly got his rocks off and kicked you out." Dex glanced Colt's way and met his stare for a moment, so Colt could see how serious Dex's next words were. "I'm not that guy." Dex looked away again as he found the masturbator in his bag. It was fully charged and ready to milk Colt all night. He slipped the device over Colt's leaking cock and powered it on. "You have no idea how well read I am. Disappearing inside books has given me an education on topics most people never bother to learn. That's how I knew how to make you have multiple orgasms with that first blow job and I can keep you on edge all night. Not only do I have the know-how to make you insane, I also have the discipline to do this all night." Colt's muscles strained. His body tensed as he tried fucking the toy on his dick.

Dex moved the device until it barely sucked on only Colt's crown. Colt growled around the gag. Dex massaged Colt's balls, ignoring the sound.

He couldn't let the subject of Clint go. Dex was still pissed off about that guy. "Do you think, even if Clint convinced you to come back, that he would ever do this for you? Do you think he could ignore his own needs and focus on making only you happy?" Dex moved the toy away, taking away Colt's pleasure. "I'm the one who does that for you." With his thumb, Dex lightly pushed upward between Colt's asshole and balls, massaging as he worked the dildo in and out. Colt strained against his restraints as cum shot from his cock, arching through the air before coating his stomach. Muffled cries caressed Dex's ears.

"We're not finished," Dex promised as he slipped the toy back over Colt's cock while it still twitched. He turned the toy on high, making the tail end of Colt's orgasm almost painful. Dex knew from experience how every sensation felt. He knew how and when to push to get the deepest pleasure. Colt would never find this with anyone else. Colt never stopped moving or moaning as the tight and fast suction dragged him closer to a second orgasm with no permission from his brain or body. Dex was in control. He would get him there.

While Colt fought against the toy sucking him off, Dex fucked him hard with the dildo. When that wasn't enough for Dex's over-stressed brain, he pulled a crop from the bag. He lightly tapped Colt's inner thighs with the crop while punishing his asshole. Dex's cock leaked and begged to be the thing stretching Colt wide. Dex couldn't go there today. He focused so hard on tormenting Colt that he didn't stop until Colt could no longer stay hard. Instead of feeling better as he stared at Colt's drained cock, he felt defeated—like he had failed in some way. Dex had left Colt completely spent, but he still didn't think Colt would ever love him the way he had loved Clint, despite his shitty treatment.

With that depressing thought making him insane on top of the growing unease inside him, Dex left Colt bound and gagged as he climbed from the bed. He gathered the toys before moving to the bathroom. He tossed them in the sink to be cleaned and changed into his pajama pants. By the time he returned to Colt, Colt stared at him in a relaxed heap. There was no love in his eyes—just as Dex suspected. He felt... ready to cover his ears and rock himself, to be honest. He set Colt's feet free first. His heart sank lower by the second. Dex's breathing got shallower. He gently tugged the ball gag, slipping it over Colt's head before tearing open the Velcro cuffs.

With Colt free, Dex sat on the edge of the bed and stared at the wall. He was a mess. It was no wonder Colt would never love him. No one could love him. He covered his ears, trying to block out the sound of the air rushing through the vents in his bedroom. It was so goddamn loud.

Colt ran his hand up Dex's spine. Dex automatically moved away from Colt's touch. He ground his back teeth and forced himself to be still as Colt's hand fell away. He swore he could feel Colt's hurt. His disappointment was just one more brick weighing Dex down and threatening to break him. He could not let that happen. Dex didn't want Colt to look at him like he was crazy on top of everything else—the way everyone who saw him fall apart did.

Colt's voice cut through the dark, sounding heavy with sadness despite Dex wearing out his body. "I think I should have come inside when you told me to on the night of the season finale, instead of getting you off in the car. That's the one and only time I truly believe you meant to make love to me. Things are so one-sided between us, Dex. I don't understand why you don't like my touch, and I don't understand why you even want me around."

Dex squeezed his eyes shut. This was hell. He couldn't stop failing. He forced words out, even though he thought his chest might cave under the pressure. "We just made love. I would never leave you unsatisfied." Heavy silence followed Dex's claim. Dex wanted to cover his ears against it again. He couldn't take much more of this tonight.

Finally, Colt sat up. A shot of panic hit Dex. He was scared as hell Colt would leave him now. "I want to touch you too." That was all the warning Dex got before Colt's lips brushed his nape. It was too much. Sensory overload hit like a heavyweight boxer. Dex couldn't breathe at all. He leapt from the bed. His gaze refused to lock on anything at all. He didn't even worry about his shirt or shoes. Dex headed for the garage as fast as his feet would take him. He had to get away. Dex needed quiet and darkness. He needed a place to decompress. Colt's feelings or reaction mattered not at all in that moment. Dex was about to come unglued and it wouldn't be pretty. He had to keep Colt safe from that.

Dex didn't stop to truly look at his surroundings until his car was parked outside his trailer. Thank God he had unconsciously chosen a place on his property. Otherwise, he might have killed someone on the road, since he didn't recall a second of the drive there. In fact, if he wasn't sitting behind the wheel, he wouldn't believe he had driven at all. Dex pushed his car door open. The trailer was waiting to be moved to the next show's location. It didn't have water or power at the moment, but he couldn't go back to the house. Colt would be through with him now. Dex just hoped he would at least stay until the morning. Dex had bought Colt a new truck and it was set to be delivered by nine a.m. tomorrow.

Before Dex made it to the door, he bent at the waist, braced his hands on his knees, and sucked air. The sound of crickets and frogs singing assailed his ears. The world was never as quiet as he needed it to be. Goddamn it. He had left Colt. Dex wanted to go back, but the rough grass beneath his feet was too much. If he couldn't handle the sensation of grass, he stood no chance against the stress of an argument. Dex just needed time and space. If Colt stayed after this, Dex would do everything within his power to be better. Tonight had just been especially bad. Between oversleeping and the noise and finding out about Clint. Then he had immediately strapped Colt down, trying to mark his territory. Fuck. He was dumb. Colt had practically begged to touch him. Who in their right mind would want Dex?

Dex straightened and tried harder to breathe normal—in and out. His head cleared a bit. Of course, the moment he could think clearly, a new wave of pain hit. He might have really just lost Colt. What was Dex supposed to do now? No doubt he would return to his old ways of paying much younger men to tolerate him while he focused solely on work. Funny how empty that thought felt now that Colt had given him a taste of real life. Damn. He didn't know how to fix this one. He wished he could be fixed.

EIGHT

COLT STARED at the brand-new Ford F-450 Limited and felt nothing. He knew, because he had been pricing new trucks not that long ago, that this one was damn near one hundred thousand dollars. It was black and beautiful. The truck had every bell and whistle imaginable. It was the exact vehicle he would have chosen for himself, and yet, Colt felt nothing. There was no joy or relief. There should have been a rush of gratitude that Dex obviously cared enough to try to make things better with a gift, but that wasn't true. Gifts were meaningless from Dex. He could blow through hundreds of thousands of dollars a day for no reason at all. This truck didn't mean Colt was special in any way. It was just a truck and Colt couldn't do this anymore.

He climbed behind the wheel, even though he shouldn't. Colt hadn't slept or even tried to sleep since Dex ran away. Dex hadn't even been wearing shoes, for fuck's sake. His wallet and phone were still on the bedside table. Colt didn't think he had gone far, but fuck if Colt knew where to look. But he knew who to ask. There was only one person Dex loved and it wasn't Colt. He rubbed his chest at the thought. It didn't matter if Dex didn't love him. Colt loved Dex and he couldn't leave him out there, dealing with whatever he was going through alone. Maybe Colt didn't know what was wrong with Dex, but he knew it was something, and he had to try to help. So Colt would go to the man Dex loved and hope he was there, even though it stung coming in second.

It didn't take much time of searching the web on the new phone Dex had bought him to find Wren's address. It was scary how easily anyone's information could be found online. Colt was thankful for that today. He drove to Wren's house on autopilot, trying not to fall in love with his new truck and its new car smell. Fucking Dex. He knew Colt too well.

Wren's house was in a quiet neighborhood and was much smaller than Colt expected. The way Dex threw his money around, Colt would have thought

Dex would have forced Wren into a home the same size as Dex's. Of course, then again, Wren was much better at standing against Dex than Colt had ever been. It was no wonder Dex had fallen for him over Colt. Colt was no one at all. He had just been in the right place at the right time to catch Dex's interest... somewhat.

Dex's car wasn't in the driveway, but the house had a big garage. Colt didn't give up hope. He forced himself to take normal and even breaths as he walked to the front door. Colt rang the doorbell before he could change his mind. After several minutes, the door swung wide. Finch was on the other side.

"It's the cowboy." He was so loud and happy to see Colt that Colt couldn't help but smile. Finch was pure and untainted joy. It was impossible to be unhappy around him.

"Hey, Finch. How have you been?" Colt took off his cowboy hat as he cleared the doorway.

Finch did his version of a nod. "I'm good. Haven is taking Wren and me to the park today. We're having a picnic and everything. I promised not to scream when the ducks get too close this time."

Colt fought the urge to laugh at the instant image that popped in his mind of Finch screaming at ducks.

"I won't hold y'all up," he promised. "I just came to talk to Wren for a second."

"Hey, Colt," Wren said, appearing inside the living room.

Colt's gaze swung Wren's way. It was like all the pain he had been barely beating back slammed into him the moment he set eyes on Wren. He couldn't compete with this guy. Hell, even Colt had tried winning Wren once upon a time.

Wren took one look at Colt and waved him into the kitchen. "Come have a seat at the table. We'll talk in here." His gaze swung Finch's way. "Give me a few and we'll go, okay, sweetie?"

"Okay."

With another nod Finch's way, Colt headed for the kitchen. Wren slid a hidden door closed behind him, keeping their conversation private. "I know that look," Wren said the moment they were alone, sounding understanding. "Dex got under your skin and now you want to know why he is the way he is."

A surprised chuckle escaped Colt as he chose a chair and sat. "Pretty much. He's also missing and I kind of hoped he might be here, but I see he isn't." He didn't stop there or slow. "The day you brought my stuff, you said you wouldn't betray his trust, but I really need to know. I know it's dumb. I should have kept my heart out of things with Dex, but I love him, and I need to know if I'm wasting my time, and what the hell is going on and—"

"He's autistic."

"What?" Colt's brain tried to catch up with Wren's bombshell as Wren filled the spot next to him at the table.

Wren nodded. "He's autistic. High functioning, obviously, but he has... quirks. Like he's a freaking artistic genius and is really amazing at analyzing situations, but he's not good at handling human interaction the way anyone else would. He's equally not good at showing or vocalizing feelings."

In his shock, Colt didn't guard his tongue. "Is that why he doesn't have sex?"

If Wren was the least bit embarrassed or uncomfortable, he didn't show it. "Yes. I think it's like a sensation slash texture thing. Like, certain touches trigger him. But I also think if you talk him through it, adding rationale to an irrational situation, he might be willing to do more. For instance, I kissed him once and he flipped, which was really confusing. It wasn't until he told me about the autism, and I thought about it that I worked out his reasoning. He had analyzed me, decided I would bolt from his life if he let our relationship get too deep and—in his mind

—he reasoned that kissing was something people do when they're in love, so we wouldn't be doing that."

"Huh," Colt grunted, taking that in. "He kisses me all the time."

A smile exploded across Wren's face. "That's because he loves you and he wants you to love him back."

Colt didn't even think. He simply spoke the truth since it was too late to go back now. "I already do, but he does shit that drives me batshit insane. Take last night as an example—sorry in advance for the TMI—but we were in bed and—I thought—closer than ever to actual sex, but then he just jumped away from me. I know he could tell he was frustrating me, but instead of talking about it, he left. And this morning," Colt said, getting louder as he got worked up all over again.

"He bought you something expensive," Wren concluded correctly.

Colt nearly leapt from his seat in his renewed irritation. "Yes. He bought me a new truck. I don't really need a new truck. I need to know what the fuck is going on."

Wren rubbed his arm, soothing him. "His mind is analytical. He also doesn't know what it's like to be anyone else. He thinks buying you things will make you happy. All he understands is how he deals with things, so you'll have to be the one who is painfully straightforward. You can't give Dex signals and hope he'll read them correctly. With Dex, you have to say, I want this. Do you want that? Can we try this? Don't do that. He's always listening and watching. He just doesn't know what he can't know. Dex has made a fuck-ton of money from doing what he loves and investing it wisely. To him, spending that money is showing his love. That's logical to him. Showing is believing. Use your words, sweetie, because he doesn't know how."

Colt nodded. It was time to man up. He could do this. "Thank you. I'm sorry to bring all this to you, but I didn't know what else to do."

Wren smacked his knee in a playful gesture. "Anytime. Seriously. Dex and I have had our ups and downs, but I love him, and I can see that you do too. I think you need each other. Don't give up."

Colt took a breath and stood. No way would he give up. Colt just needed someone to point him in the right direction. He hoped Wren was right about Dex needing words, because Colt was about to drown him in them. It was time to be all in or get out —for both of them. His determination faded as reality sank in. "I don't know how to find him. He didn't take his phone or anything."

Wren made a dismissive motion and dug his phone from his pocket. "Did he take the Bentley?"

Colt nodded and Wren toyed with his phone.

After a moment, Wren turned the device Colt's way, and pointed to a tiny red spot on the digital map on his phone. "He's at the trailer. It's parked on the west side of his property. That's where it's stored between shoots."

Thank god for Wren's efficiency at keeping up with Dex or Colt would be trapped in his worry all day. Colt pushed to his feet. "Thank you. I really appreciate all your help." While Colt knew more words were exchanged between them, his brain was already headed to get his man. Nothing else mattered and Colt had to make Dex see that. Colt couldn't lose the only person he had left. He wouldn't survive it.

DEX STARED AT NOTHING, SEEING NOTHING. HE knew Colt's new truck had to have been delivered. Dex wondered if he liked it or if he had even been there to accept the delivery. It was possible Colt had already left him. Dex's eyes fell closed at the thought. All he wanted was for Colt to be happy. That was it. He just wanted him to smile. Dex should let him go. Set Colt free. There was no way Colt was happy being with him, and Dex was out of ideas. Maybe he simply wasn't capable of making someone else happy long term or in a real relationship. It was possible that was something that was beyond his skill set. Maybe empty gifts was all he would ever be to anyone.

The door to his trailer opened and Colt stepped inside. Hope soared in Dex's chest until he caught sight of Colt's expression. Colt still wore the same expression he had last night—like he had made a mistake by choosing a life with Dex. Damn.

"Hello there, beautiful cowboy. Did you get my gift?"

Colt didn't answer. Instead, he crossed the room and stood to hover over Dex. "This has to stop."

Pain punched Dex right in the heart. He swallowed, trying to stay calm. It wasn't Colt's fault Dex was the way he was. "If that's what you want, I'll tell everyone it was my fault the wedding is off."

A sexy growl rumbled in Colt's throat. "You're not even understanding me." Colt said, sounding like the words were more for himself. "Fine," he said, obviously deciding to change tactics. "I can have this conversation one-sided. I love you."

Dex blinked, unsure if he heard correctly.

Colt didn't stop to let him catch up. "Do you love me?"

"Yes." Dex had assumed that was obvious.

Colt gave him a sharp nod. "I need you to tell me things like that. I need the words."

"I love you," Dex repeated dutifully.

A tiny smile appeared on Colt's lips and hope washed over Dex for the first time. "I don't want things to change between us. Okay? I want to marry you. But I also need us to be a real couple."

Dex was confused again. "We are a real couple."

"See," Colt said, sounding irritated again. "I thought so too, but you don't talk to me about things. When I try, like last night, you run away. So I want to talk about some things."

"Okay," Dex said, even though he had a bad feeling he wouldn't be very good at Colt's definition of a real relationship.

Colt dropped to his haunches between Dex's knees. He massaged Dex's thighs while holding Dex's stare. "Do you trust me, baby?"

Dex didn't hesitate. "Of course."

A sweet smile touched Colt's lips. "Then please

tell me when I'm doing something you don't like." His smile grew as he added, "Or when I'm doing something you do like. Trust that I love you enough to handle you at your worst and your best. Just believe in us, okay?"

"I do."

Colt's smile turned sardonic. "Do you? Then come to bed with me right now."

Without thought, Dex sucked in a quick and ragged breath. He was about to fail Colt on every level when he freaked again. The thing was, he loved Colt and he didn't want to lose him. So he stood. "Okay."

As Colt came to his feet as well, he took Dex's hand. Dex let Colt lead him down the short hall to the bedroom. Before panic could fully set in, Colt climbed onto the bed, settled onto his back, and didn't move. "You're in charge, sexy. I'm yours to do with as you please."

The tightness in Dex's chest eased. Colt was too amazing to stay in the dark. Dex wrapped the strength around him that Colt gave him with his love and leapt. "I'm autistic. I didn't want to melt down in front of you last night. That's why I came here." Colt didn't even flinch beneath Dex's confession. Instead, he still looked like home to Dex. Safe. Dex found himself climbing onto the bed next to him and baring his heart. "It doesn't happen often anymore. Luckily, I've done a good job of surrounding myself with the familiar and keeping a routine that keeps me secure. Yesterday, I let myself get too stressed after the break in my routine. You didn't do anything wrong. I can't have you thinking that."

Colt chewed his bottom lip and nodded. "You scared me," he admitted after a moment, making Dex's heart sink. "I thought maybe I made you feel trapped with me and maybe you just needed to get away from me—like I was suffocating you and you couldn't get away fast enough."

"No, baby," Dex rushed to reassure him. "In fact, when I got here, I immediately missed you and I spent the rest of the night wishing I wasn't like this. Wishing this awful thing away before it destroys us. That much self-hatred hasn't hit me in years. I didn't go to bed at all. I just sat here, hoping you would stay."

Colt rolled into a sitting position and snagged Dex's waist. He urged Dex to straddle his lap. There was so much love in Colt's eyes that Dex could barely breathe. "There is no chance this could destroy us. In fact, this is a nonissue as far as I'm concerned. I love you. Melt down if you need to, because I'm not going anywhere. I also don't expect you to do anything you're not comfortable doing. I'm sorry. I just wanted you to tell me what's going on with you and I knew you wouldn't if I didn't force your hand. If you want to go home now, we can." Colt shrugged. "I just want to be with you in any capacity you'll have me. Sex means next to nothing in comparison to just holding you."

Something shifted in Dex's chest. He hadn't meant to make Colt feel like his touch was unwanted. Years ago, Dex had dated a guy named Rylan. They had never been more than a good time —like all Dex's so-called relationships had been. Rylan had warned Dex that Dex would meet someone someday who would knock him on his ass and make him wonder why he was incapable of looking at another soul. Colt was that person for him. While Dex had known that all along, he realized now that knowledge had made Dex treat Colt differently. He had hidden himself, hoping Colt could love him—not for who he was, but for what he could pretend to be for Colt's sake. Never in the past had he cared what anyone thought. Now that he did, Dex didn't know how to act. All he knew was what Wren taught him and what Colt confirmed he needed—Dex could use his words.

"I very much would like to make love to you. If you're not in a hurry to get away from me, that is."

Colt's arms tightened around Dex, drawing him closer. "There's nowhere I'd rather be than right here with you."

"I need to be in control."

A wicked-looking smile curved Colt's lips. Up close, his eyes looked devilish as they crinkled in the corners. "If you haven't noticed, I like it when you're in charge."

"Good." Dex urged Colt back down on the bed as he lowered his voice to a whisper. "Don't touch me. Okay?"

Colt gave a small nod. It was enough. With his weight braced on his hands and knees, Dex lowered his head and touched his lips to Colt's chin. It was only a light kiss before he moved lower, kissing Colt's throat. He felt more than heard Colt's breath catch. Dex inhaled, savoring the moment as his fingers went to work on Colt's jeans. He undid the button and slid down his zipper. As he peeled Colt's jeans down his hips, an image of Colt, restrained and squirming, floated through Dex's mind. He had almost been completely out of his head during their playtime yesterday. Today, he was better.

"Are you sore from yesterday?"

Colt boldly held his stare. There was no shame in his eyes. "I'm not too sore for this."

Even though that wasn't the answer Dex wanted, he could work with that. Yesterday had been about Dex's need to escape his mind. Today was about making love to the man who would be his husband. After removing Colt's pants, Dex pressed his lips to Colt's hipbone. He inhaled Colt's scent before moving higher. Dex pushed Colt's shirt higher as he kissed his way back to Colt's mouth. He peeled the shirt up and over Colt's head before capturing his lips. Their slow and sweet kiss matched the way Dex wanted to move inside Colt. They kissed until Colt was breathless beneath him. Only then did Dex move away. He stood. At the edge of the bed, Dex held Colt's stare and stripped. Sunlight poured through the tiny window in the room. The window's dark tint did nothing to help cool the trailer from the heat blasting inside from the hot sun with no electricity for air. A faint sheen of sweat coated Colt's skin, making Dex's mouth water. He loved the way Colt tasted. The bright bedroom also made it impossible to hide the scars he normally kept covered. Colt's gaze moved over Dex's body. If he saw any flaws, Dex couldn't see it in his expression. Colt looked ready to beg.

As much as Dex loved it when Colt pled for release, today wasn't for that. Dex found the condoms and lube that had been stashed in the drawer by the bed for God only knows how long. Dex couldn't recall the last time he had needed them. While Colt watched his every move, Dex suited and lubed up before crawling onto the bed. Once again, he couldn't help but linger at Colt's hip, kissing him. Dex had more of an oral fixation than he wanted to admit. He absolutely lived to suck dick. For some people, it was a chore. Dex fought the urge to suck Colt all day every day. Kissing the man's hip was as close as he could let himself get at the moment.

By the time he settled between Colt's thighs and captured his mouth, he could feel how Colt fought not to touch him. Dex knew him, though. He would obey. Colt was a good boy all the way to his soul. Their tongues stroked and Colt fought to get closer with his tongue, proving how badly he needed more. Dex urged Colt's knees higher and probed at his ass. Between their playtime yesterday and worrying he had lost Colt, Dex was already on edge. He swore he saw stars as his crown pressed past the tight ring of muscles surrounding Colt's asshole. He gasped for air as he sank deeper inside Colt's body. The low and long moan Colt released nearly crippled Dex. He was turned on past the point of painful. The moment he was fully seated, Dex changed angles and rocked.

He knew exactly where to hit to get the most reaction from Colt. Colt did not disappoint. He ripped his mouth away and cried Dex's name in that begging tone Dex couldn't withstand. Dex dug his knees into the mattress, pressed his forehead to Colt's sternum, and went to work. The sound of skin slapping skin mixed with their ragged breathing as Dex pounded inside Colt. All thoughts of going slow disappeared. With his eyes squeezed shut, Dex focused solely on pounding that button that would drive Colt insane. When he felt Colt's muscles tense, Dex wrapped his arms around Colt's thighs and held on for the ride as he moved faster and pounded harder. Sweat poured down his body and his muscles screamed. Nothing mattered but the building pressure. Colt's body stiffened so hard and fast that he nearly broke off Dex's dick before the first spasm hit. When Colt's body convulsed in a powerful orgasm, he sucked Dex deeper, dragging a cry from his throat. He blew. Dex didn't stop pumping or crying out in pleasure until the last twitch. He open-mouth-kissed every place he could reach on Colt's body, trying to consume him in every way.

"Jesus. I love you. Goddamn. I want to touch you."

"It's okay. You can touch me. I love you too," Dex whispered as he came down hard on Colt's mouth. He sucked and licked, savoring the weight of Colt's arms as they encircled him. Dex fell into a gasping heap, half sprawled across Colt's chest. Colt brought Dex's hand to his mouth, kissing his palm, wrist, and forearm. Anywhere he could reach.

"Goddamn," Colt gasped, sounding breathless. "I should've known you would steal my soul when you finally made love to me. It's unfair for one person to be so damn good at everything."

A laugh rose in Dex's throat. Happiness washed over him like a tidal wave. He wasn't sure he was as good as Colt was easily impressed. Or maybe they were magical together. He hadn't decided. All Dex knew was he didn't want to move. It was hot as hell in their tiny bedroom, but Dex didn't care to be anywhere else. Time passed. Their breathing slowed. Everything went quiet inside Dex's head while Colt held him and toyed with his fingers. He kissed another path down Dex's forearm. Colt went still for a moment before holding Dex's arm away from him and inspecting it.

"Jesus, baby. Who did this to you? These bite

mark scars look like someone bit all the way through the skin."

Dex fought the urge to yank his arm away. "Why do you think I don't like to break down? Biting is an impulse I can't control when I get too far gone."

Colt gently moved Dex's arm back to his mouth. He placed light kisses on the scars. "I'll take care of you. You can trust me to keep you safe."

The burn behind Dex's eyes was out of his control. His mom was the only person to ever see him come unglued to the point of hurting himself. She had always taken care of him and tried to find healthier ways for him to cope. He never believed anyone else would want that job. Colt didn't sound scared. Still, Dex tried to reassure him. "You don't have to worry. I'm not as bad as I was when I was younger. I have different oral fixations these days."

A sexy-sounding chuckle caressed Dex's ears. "I want to hear all about your life," Colt said suddenly, taking Dex by surprise. He rolled, pinning Dex beneath him as he focused on Dex with so much excitement in his eyes, Dex would have given him anything in that moment. "Now that you've let me in, I want everything. I need to know every detail of the years I missed."

That was a lot. Dex didn't know where to start.

"Can I hit the highlights? Every detail seems a bit much."

Colt chuckled. The happiness in the sound made Dex's heart smile. Colt nodded. "Hit the highlights and I'll ask in-depth questions if need be."

That seemed fair. Dex picked a place and dove in while Colt settled down with his head on Dex's chest. "Well, as you pointed out not that long ago, I was raised by a single mother. Obviously, I have a father, I suppose, but I never knew his name. It's not on my birth certificate, and—honestly—I never cared enough to ask. I figured if he didn't want my mom—who was the greatest person to ever live—then he damn sure wouldn't want me. I went to public school in the day when kids like me were sequestered from the normal kids." He fought the urge to do air quotes around normal. Some bitterness ran deep. Instead, he focused on sticking to the facts and leaving his emotions out of things. "Being different automatically made me a target of bullying. For the most part, I survived by keeping to myself and writing." Dex went back to those days in his mind. He had been so angry and lonely. Dex was pragmatic enough to realize he had become who he was today because of those terrible times. He didn't mind sharing that part of himself with Colt.

"I would watch the popular kids flirt and win. Life looked so easy for them. So I would create these challenges for them in my head, humbling them and turning them against each other. Much like your game, the story grew bigger until I had several volumes. After graduation, I caught a break and got an unpaid internship at a local TV station. I bagged groceries and wrangled carts at night to make enough money to pay for my car and insurance. Mom never seemed to mind if I stayed living with her forever and I was in no hurry to leave." That was the point in Dex's life where things took a turn.

Dex held Colt closer where he could keep talking without fear of Colt looking at him while he did. "Mom died right after I turned twenty. She just went to sleep one night and didn't wake up. Her heart just stopped. Luckily, she had enough life insurance through her factory job that I could afford to bury her and finish paying off the house she left me. But then, the real loneliness set in. I started taking my lunch breaks at the TV station outside and went back to writing again. For a few months, I think I just sort of disappeared inside it. One day, this man came outside to smoke, and he asked what I was writing about. I blushed and stammered as I told him a little about my story. The more interest he showed, the more I told. He said, 'Well, I'm sold. How much do you want for it?'" Dex smiled again at the memory. Sometimes he missed the innocence of it all. "The rest is pretty much history. I sold my first show and then the next and then the next until I was eventually financing them and taking a more hands-on approach."

"So your mom didn't live to see you become a star. That's heartbreaking."

It was, but he couldn't think about that. "It's your turn. Tell me everything."

Colt chuckled at the demand, obviously realizing how big the job was to recount his whole life. "My life has been pretty much the opposite of yours. My dad works on an oil rig, which is dangerous, so it pays really well. My mom is an RN and equally makes good money. I grew up in a nice house on a huge farm. While I had to work it every day, I would still say I was thoroughly spoiled. I drove a nice truck and went to the best schools. Played football," Colt added, like that should have been obvious, and it was. Dex lost himself in the cadence of Colt's voice.

"My life was as normal and apple pie as could be, and then I grew up. I could've gone to college, but I decided to take a year off because I hated school. A year turned into two when a friend of mine suggested we take up bronco riding. It was a rush and I was addicted. One day, I had this open future where I could've done and been anything. The next, I was partying, traveling, drinking, and betting deep. Everything kept spiraling until I met Clint. It was like hitting a brick wall and getting bounced back into reality. The partying and traveling stopped." Colt paused. Dex heard him swallow, as if the memories hurt.

"The drinking and the betting didn't stop, though. Clint would sort of twist me into wagering on things while giving me just enough attention to keep me hanging on. The drinking got worse each time I realized how far down I'd let myself get. Then my parents stopped taking my calls. I finally broke down and went to see my mom at work. I threw myself on her mercy and begged to come home, hoping to free myself of the mess I'd made. She cried and told me she loved me enough to let me go." Colt fell silent and Dex waited. It hurt his chest to think of Colt being cut loose from his family. No doubt Colt had done a lot of things in his drinking days to make them feel like they had to cut ties before he drowned them, but damn. Colt had changed and Dex doubted they knew it.

Colt cleared his throat. It sounded painful.

"Anyhow, I went to rehab not long after that. Clint showed up one day and offered to pay off the rehab center and all my gambling debts if I would come live on the ranch and work. I didn't have anyone else, and as you said, the rest is history."

For a long time, they stayed quiet while holding each other. Dex tried to think of a way to comfort Colt, but all he knew to do was try to make Colt's life better than it had been. "I love you." The words slipped so easily from Dex. He wondered why he hadn't said them before today. While they had butted heads a lot over the past year, Colt had never truly shut him down or out. He wasn't the type to back down from a challenge. Being with Dex would always be hard work, but Dex would make it worthwhile.

Colt came up onto his elbow. He nudged Dex's chin higher with his fingertips, forcing Dex to meet his stare. "I love you too." His thumb stroked Dex's bottom lip, but his eyes never wavered from holding Dex's stare. With anyone else, that would have been uncomfortable. Dex liked it when Colt looked at him. Then Colt's expression turned sad. "You're all I have. Please don't hide things or run away from me again."

Dex couldn't deny him. "I won't, but I'm not all you have."

A heartbreaking smile touched Colt's lips. "You are."

Understood. Colt wouldn't be inviting his parents back into his life. "I guess it's a good thing I probably love you enough for twenty people."

Colt's smile grew, turning genuine. "You are an overachiever."

He was, and Dex would never let Colt feel alone or shut out again. Some things were too precious to lose. Dex could live without a lot of things and people, but Colt wasn't on that list. They were each other's family now. Dex wouldn't let Colt down.

NINE

MAYBE IT WAS RIDICULOUS, but because of Dex, the sun shone brighter than it had in years for Colt. Colt was pretty sure he was just trapped in a dream. He smiled at the ridiculous idea as he let his arm dangle into the pool's water as the float slowly drifted around the pool. On his stomach, he stared at the water, transfixed, seeing nothing but the images in his mind. Colt fought against the out-of-control grin that had been pulling at his lips since Dex took over his life. Countless times he had caught himself smiling so hard, his face hurt for no reason at all. He felt a bit stupid, but Dex made him that way. As much as Colt wanted to claim that Dex had swept him away that day he had offered Colt the full-time position being his, that wasn't true. Colt had been fighting against his feelings since the day they met almost a year ago. Dex was alluring and larger than life. Colt had never met anyone like him, except he worried he had. At first, he had feared Dex would be exactly like Clint, and so he had fought hard not to feel what his heart demanded. Now that Colt knew he had been wrong about Dex, all the feelings he had fought so hard to suppress wouldn't be squelched. Dex was unmatched. Colt never wanted to come up for air, especially since Dex hadn't budged from his side since the first exchanged I love you.

"Obviously, Toby knows I'm no longer interested in their services at Cubs for Rent, yet he has still sent us an invite to a party this weekend." Colt turned his head and watched as Dex walked to the edge of the pool, holding a card.

Possessiveness roiled in Colt's gut. "He must want me to go to jail. No one else gets to have you but me."

Dex's bland expression rarely budged. Now was no different. He nodded. "That was my thought as well, so I almost tossed it. Since your name was listed too, it caught my attention enough to open it. Turns out, it's an invitation to a fundraiser for a charity that Finch wants to start."

The out-of-control smile was back. This time,

Colt gave himself permission to indulge by lying to himself that it was for Finch. "Really? What sort of charity is Finch starting? Cerebral palsy research?"

A rare smile touched Dex's lips. "That was my first thought, as well, but no. Puppy mill rescue."

Somehow, Colt's smile grew even bigger. "That kid is too precious for this world."

"Agreed," Dex said, setting the invitation aside and slipping into the water with Colt. "Luckily, he's also surrounded by adults with the means to encourage his dreams. So, what do you say, gorgeous cowboy? Should we accept?"

"Of course. We can't miss that."

Dex scooped a handful of water onto Colt's back, cooling him down. He had the most beautiful eyes. Colt couldn't stop staring at them while Dex focused on his task of wetting Colt's skin. His cold hand landed on the back of Colt's overheated thigh, right below his swim trunks. Dex's fingers slipped beneath the material. Colt's cock twitched. Before Dex, it had taken a lot more to turn him on than the simple brush of fingers on the back of his thigh. But now, it was Dex, and Colt's body knew what Dex could do for it. There was no unlearning Dex's skill.

"You're such a temptation," Dex said, sounding as if the words were more for himself than Colt. "I don't think for one second you're trying to seduce me by displaying yourself on this float, but still all I want is to see how well you can hold your balance while I spread you wide and eat your ass."

Colt sucked in a desperate-sounding breath. "Jesus." Colt meant the curse from the bottom of his soul. He swore he could already feel Dex's tongue. As Dex's fingertips curled around the waistband of Colt's swim trunks, Colt wrapped both arms around the float and held on. Even if he drowned, Colt had no intention of missing this. Dex could make a man scream more than a rollercoaster. Colt was always up for the ride.

EACH TIME DEX RUINED COLT'S PLANS TO BE lazy for the day, he swore he would do better the next time. It seemed there would never be a next time that didn't tempt Dex to seduce Colt.

After making Colt cum in the pool and nearly drowning him in the process, they had barely made it inside the pool house before Colt was ass up with his face buried in the loveseat and Dex's cock buried in his ass. It was a good thing they were getting married and would never be with anyone else again because condoms had gone to the wayside a long time ago. They were too greedy and couldn't keep their hands to themselves. Just as Dex had grown to love Colt looking at him, he had come to crave Colt's touch. His demands that Colt stay hands off until Dex's mind could take the overload were less and less all the time. While he would always have days when he couldn't withstand noise or physical contact, Colt was already part of Dex's routine. It was a bit terrifying when Dex looked too closely at things. When his mom had died, his routine had been shredded, leaving him in a place mentally he almost hadn't recovered. For a while, he thought he might have to live in a home as Finch once had, incapable of caring for himself. Now, he worried—if anything should happen to Colt—Dex might finally cross that line. He hadn't wanted to depend on anyone this much again. Loving Colt was worth the risk. Plus, it was out of his control anyhow.

Sprawled across Colt's chest, Dex listened to Colt's steady heartbeat while soaking up the affection he couldn't live without. Only the fact that he was as necessary to Colt as Colt was to him kept Dex from worrying too much.

"You know," Colt said, startling Dex. He thought Colt had fallen asleep. "Sometimes, I worry when filming starts back that you'll get sick of having me underfoot in that tiny trailer. Other times, I wonder if you'll get anything done with me keeping you distracted."

Dex didn't need to think about it. "I managed last season. Maybe you weren't living with me, but you were mentally underfoot, keeping me distracted."

A sexy rumble of laughter vibrated against his ear. "Do you think Becca has spent that full million on liquor yet?"

Dex couldn't stop smiling. Colt's brain was a beautiful place. Even though he openly disliked Becca, Dex didn't doubt for a second he was still worrying over what happened to her. "I think Becca will end up working in porn and be just fine, even if she has blown through her money already."

Colt stroked Dex's back, making his eyelids grow heavy. "You'd make a great porn star," Colt said, startling a laugh from Dex. "I could see you doing those videos with the rubber suits and milking machines." Dex laughed harder at the image Colt painted. The harder he laughed, the more ridiculous Colt became. "You'd be like, here's a plastic straw to breathe with, bitch. I hope you like dragon dong because I've got one of those too."

Dex covered his face and snorted. "Oh my god. I'm not that bad."

Colt's arms tightened around him. "I don't know," he said, sounding serious. "You have a lot of unexpected shit in that duffel bag. Every time I think I've seen all that could possibly be inside, you bring out something else."

With his lips pressed together, Dex tried not to laugh. Colt had no idea. Dex had ordered more shit the other day. Their last playtime had been nothing. Dex fully intended to rock Colt's world this next time. He imagined, once Colt broke, it would be a beautiful sight. Maybe this time, he would forgo the ball gag so he could hear Colt scream. Damn, maybe the trailer would be a little too small after all. The walls were paper thin. Maybe Dex would just stay home this next season. Colt kept his creative juices flowing right here. They could have so much fun.

TEN

FOR AS LONG AS Colt could remember, he had been the type who sought the wallflowers and befriended the people sitting alone. Something about quiet people who didn't need to be loud and flashy called to Colt. Which was only funny because Colt had fallen hard in love with the brightest star in the room. That was a fact that events—like this one Cubs for Rent was holding for Finch's charity—highlighted for him. While everyone under the sun stopped Dex, trying to steal a moment of his time, Colt headed straight for a young guy sitting alone by the open French doors. He was tiny and had a head full of soft-looking brown curls. Despite sitting alone, his unnaturally blue gaze boldly held Colt's stare as he closed the distance between them. The closer he got, the smaller the guy seemed. Colt felt an odd desire to sit close and keep him safe from a crowd of predatory men.

Deep dimples and a wicked smile met Colt as he came to stand over the man. Colt blinked in surprise at the boldness of such a small and shy-looking guy. "Hello, there." The guy motioned toward the empty chair beside him. "Would you like to join me on the fringes where it's quiet?"

"Please," Colt said, claiming the chair. "I'm Colt," Colt said as he sat.

Another impish smile flashed his way. "Hudson." The name didn't fit at all, but Colt nodded.

"Nice to meet you, Hudson."

"You, as well, Colt." Colt had no idea why, but he felt as if Hudson was laughing at him. Hudson's gaze locked on to him again. "Do you work for Cubs for Rent?"

Colt shook his head. "I almost did, but my life took a turn. What about you?"

"Yes, since the beginning."

Silence fell between them and Colt chose to enjoy the slight breeze slipping through the open door while keeping an eye on Dex. Now that Colt truly knew him, Colt realized how blind he had once been. Dex never looked directly at anyone. To the ignorant eye, he looked rude and uncaring. Instead, Dex was probably the most caring person in the room. He felt deeply about everything. His inability to look at anyone was something out of his control. He was uncomfortable. Once he knew someone, looking them in the eye got easier. Colt felt special for being invited inside Dex's small circle of trust. A smile kept tugging at the corners of his mouth as he watched people jockey to be exactly where Colt was —under Dex's protection.

"Is that your man?" Hudson asked, pulling Colt from his lovesick musings.

Heat filled Colt's face for getting caught in the depths of his lovesick mooning. "Yes. If he ever frees himself, I'll introduce you." A horrible thought hit Colt. Dex had done some hiring of escorts over the years. "Unless you already know him."

An adorable chuckle caressed Colt's ears. "No. I don't really know anyone here. Even though I work for Cubs for Rent, I'm not listed on their site. Working through the Kodiak brothers saves me from the hassle of self-employment taxes, but I'm actually under exclusive contract with someone. I have been for..." Hudson looked thoughtful for a second before finishing. "...three years, I suppose."

That was a long time to be nothing more than a

contract. Colt wasn't rude enough to say that. It was also a long time for someone who looked so young. "Is he here?"

Hudson shook his head and gave Colt a little shrug. "He doesn't leave his house. It's not unusual for me to do things like this alone. Cage sends me with a check, and I sit in the corner all night. It's boring, but I'm not much of a socializer."

Colt was beyond curious. He had a million intrusive questions—like was this guy eighty or did he suffer from agoraphobia? If he was afraid to leave his house, how did he afford Hudson? Colt was frozen by his overwhelming need to know everything.

"Look out," Hudson said, pulling Colt from his thoughts. "Incoming. This one looks desperate."

Colt followed Hudson's line of gaze without thought. Clint—dressed to the nines and completely focused on Colt—headed his way. "Fuck." That was the only word Colt managed before Clint was there, hovering over him and looking every bit as desperate as Hudson accused. Colt's brain refused to acknowledge what he was seeing. Clint was here. This was an event attended by prominently gay men. Hell had one hundred percent frozen over when he hadn't been looking.

"Colt."

His hatred doubled in a flash of red across his vision. Years. Colt had literally spent years wishing Clint would accept his sexuality and stop pretending Colt was his employee. Now, here he was—like all the pain he caused with his secrets never happened.

Clint spun the cowboy hat held between his hands in a nervous gesture when Colt didn't respond. He cleared his throat. His gaze slid Hudson's way and back again. He cleared his throat again. "May I speak to you in private?"

"I'll go," Hudson offered before Colt could find his voice.

"What could you possibly have to say to him in private?" Dex asked, appearing from nowhere.

Hudson was half out of his seat. His gaze slid between all parties. He sat back down. "I can't wait to tell Cage this one," he muttered to himself as he settled in, obviously intent on watching the show.

Clint barely spared Dex a quick glance. "Get lost, Dex. Colt is a grown man. He can decide for himself. You're not married to him yet."

Colt's hackles rose at how dismissive Clint was of their engagement, as if love really meant nothing to him. As if Colt would ever choose Clint over Dex. Colt stood and brushed Clint aside. In his irritation, he became the liar. "Actually, we are already married, and I won't disrespect my husband by speaking with you anywhere, much less in private. Excuse us." Colt gave Hudson a small nod, silently offering his goodbye before taking Dex's hand and walking away. If Clint made any attempt to stop him, Colt missed it. Dex had his full focus.

Hudson's voice followed them. "Oh, that's too bad. Nothing exciting ever happens at these parties. I don't know why Cage forces me to come to these things."

"Well, that's a pity," Dex said, his voice heavy with humor. "I really wanted to throw you the wedding of the century, but now it looks like a quick trip to visit a judge I know instead."

A chuckle rose in Colt's throat. Dex could not tolerate a single lie, and Colt loved this man. "Sorry about that. I guess I saw red when he acted as if you're disposable." Colt pulled Dex to a stop and tugged Dex into his arms, leaving Dex no other choice but to meet his stare. Wren's advice about being the one with the words raced to the surface. He would never stop giving Dex everything he had to give. "I need you to know there's no one else out there for me. Strip away the money and fame and I still think you're the greatest man alive. I hope that you know that."

Dex's mouth lifted in one corner. "Does that mean you'll throw away your cowboy hat?"

A snort escaped Colt. "You can still go fuck yourself on that one. My grandpa gave me that hat."

Dex's gaze dropped to Colt's mouth for a second before returning to hold his stare. "I'm only playing with you. It's sexy when you defy me. How about we toss all your old clothes, then?"

"No. In fact, I might start wearing them again. You fell for me in those clothes."

"Mhmm," Dex said, making Colt's smile grow. "Admittedly, I do miss the tight Wranglers, but the shirts have to go. You're way too sexy to be hiding behind such a scratchy material." His hands ran up Colt's chest. "This body deserves expensive things."

Every thought about where they were flew from Colt's head. All he saw was Dex. His hands automatically found Dex's ass, pulling him closer. "If that's the case, from now on, I should only wear you."

Dex brushed his lips across Colt's. "I like this plan, Mr. Wise."

"Goddamn." The breathless-sounding curse escaped Colt without thought. "Sorry. That just sounded too amazing rolling from your lips. It caught me off guard. How did this happen?" The question was every bit as much out of his control as the curse had been. He didn't understand how they had gone so quickly from nothing to everything. One day, Colt had wanted to throttle Dex. The next, he couldn't imagine his life without him. Surely there had been some things in between, but all Colt knew was the all-consuming love.

"Do you think Wren would be upset if I gave him a check and swept you away?"

Colt couldn't stop smiling. "I think Wren is too busy tonight to worry about us. What do you have in mind?"

Dex made a sexy humming noise that stole the air from Colt's lungs. "I'm thinking a quickie marriage and a slow fuck in a town where no one knows our names."

It was like Christmas morning. Dex always dangled Colt's biggest dreams in front of him like an irresistible carrot. "I'm thinking I should have lost my temper with Clint a long time ago."

"We should go, Mr. Wise."

Damn. Dex couldn't say it too many times to appease Colt's needy soul. Just as the first time Dex had made him an offer he couldn't refuse; Colt was sold with zero regrets or second thoughts. They would have a wonderful life together filled with creativity and laughter. Filled with love. Colt couldn't wait to get started.

Keep an eye out for the next Cubs for Rent, *After Cage.*

ABOUT THE AUTHOR

Charity Parkerson is an award winning and multi-published author with several companies. Born with no filter from her brain to her mouth, she decided to take this odd quirk and insert it in her characters.

*Eight-time Readers' Favorite Award Winner
    *2015 Passionate Plume Award Finalist
    *2013 Reviewers' Choice Award Winner
    *2012 ARRA Finalist for Favorite Paranormal Romance
    *Five-time winner of The Mistress of the Darkpath

Connect with her online:

--Join   my   street   team:
facebook.com/TeamCharityParkerson
    --Website: charityparkerson.com
    --Facebook:
facebook.com/authorCharityParkerson

facebook.com/TheMenofSin

--Twitter: twitter.com/CharityParkerso

A spoiled billionaire meets a lowly ranch hand and sparks fly... in more ways than one.

Dex Wise is the billionaire playboy everyone dreams of winning. Until they meet him, that is. Dex is spoiled and vain. The number of people he cares about can be counted on one hand and only takes one finger. He's never met anyone who doesn't have a price. Life bored him to tears years ago. The only things he feels any passion about are the TV shows he creates. Those are his babies. He won't let anything ruin that love, especially not the problems of some stubborn ranch hand named Colt who is way too sexy and stubborn for his own good.

When Colt started his job at Crooked Creek Ranch, he never expected his duties would include babysitting twenty drunk college students for some rich guy's reality show. While he might not have any choice in the matter, he'll be damned if he lets Dex Wise completely own him. If that means he has to sell his time through Cubs for Rent to free himself from the ranch that already owns him, then so be it. He just wished Dex wasn't so incredibly sexy. That seems a bit unfair.

When Dex makes Colt an offer he can't refuse, their passionate personalities don't disappear when Colt signs on the dotted line. But with the way they keep ending up in bed together, it is only a matter of time before someone breaks.

ISBN 9781946099631

90000

9 781946 099631

CHARITYPARKERSON.COM